LANCER; HERO OF THE WEST

The El Paso Affair

by

Bob Brill

I0536932

Lancer; Hero of the West – The El Paso Affair is a work of historical fiction. Many of the important historical events, figures and locations are as accurately portrayed as possible. In keeping with a work of fiction, various events and occurrences were invented by the author.

ISBN: 978-0-692-08647-6

Cover design: Julia Chandrasekaran, Designer*Friendly

DEDICATION AND ACKNOWLEDGEMENTS

This book is dedicated to the modern-day Western balladeers, such as Marty Robbins, who kept the Western genre alive with music that inspired a generation. It was during a turbulent time he made it easier for us to remember the pioneer spirit which was the Old West, and helped restore a part of us which was in danger of being lost. For the words and the music we are grateful.

Many thanks to Wendy, a sharp-eyed and diligent book editor; to my daughter Julia for her immensely important and wonderful work on the covers of my books (and without whom I am lost); to my dad, who inspired in me a love for the West; and to my beautiful wife Paula, who inspires me every day of my life.

FOREWORD

Every man grows during his lifetime. Lancer, our hero is no different. Readers of this series will notice his growth and changes in this adventure.

The changes may be subtle to some, more obvious to others. Growth is good. Change is constant. I reveal more of Lancer's personal story in this novel, as I have done in each previous episode. My hope is you enjoy the voice of the story and want to read the other books.

Those drawn to the nostalgia and charm of the Old West will understand why this book is dedicated to the Western balladeers, especially Marty Robbins. The main character of *Lancer, Hero of the West* is a compilation of 1950s TV Western heroes, as well as my own imagination. Marty Robbins was teaching us about the West through popular music during then. In reading these pages you may find yourself reminiscing, thinking about those songs.

From "El Paso" to the later "El Paso City," "Big Iron" and "Saddle Tramp," the enduring music of that great Western singer has touched us all. It still leaves a powerful impression on those who enjoy tales of the Old West as America was expanding from sea to sea.

 Thank you, Marty.

CHAPTER ONE

Daybreak arrived gray and dusty in Tombstone as Lancer stirred. He was alone this morning as he lay in his bed. The sheets were smooth and the covers warm, and while he was unaccustomed to waking up alone, this didn't feel bad.

Suddenly he felt a twinge in his spirit. Something was up. He didn't know what, or who might be involved, but he didn't like what he was feeling. He slowly got out of bed and couldn't shake that strange feeling. As his sleepiness wore off, a premonition formed in his brain. Some history-making event was about to happen in his corner of the universe, and he was not going to be a part of it.

Lancer knew something about history. He loved it and he had lived it. Bull Run had been his moment to shine. As a young officer in the Union Army, he would turn the tide for his unit in that awful war... not unlike another young Civil War hero by the name of George Armstrong Custer, who would later follow a different path, one that led to infamy. Lancer, too, had moved on after the war, seeking his own way of dealing with the horrors and the aftermath of a bloody four-year campaign that divided a nation.

His travels as a child to Europe with his father, his time spent in the Orient, and his family's business, which took him as a youngster to all parts east of the Mississippi, made him appreciate the past as much as look forward to the future. But the ominous feeling he was having this morning did not make him feel happy about the future. He had a vague sense of dread that whatever history was in the making, it would not be good.

He looked at his pocket watch and saw it was half past six. He needed coffee but knew it would be another half hour before his manservant, Javier, would bring breakfast. Eggs and bacon would taste mighty good this morning, he mused as he moved over to the window to look down on Tombstone's main street. A few cowboys were milling around but it was way too early for the ladies of the town to be strolling and gazing into the new stores that were popping up in the growing town.

Indeed, Tombstone was bustling these days. Enterprising businessmen in Europe had cut deals with local merchants who were eager to bring in goods for their customers. Those customers, in turn, were anxious to spend their hard-dug silver. These were new and exciting times for everyone, it seemed. The ladies of the night were always looking for easy prey, especially a miner who had pulled enough out of the ground to repay his backers and move forward.

Lancer's friend Wyatt Earp had pooled his resources with his brothers -- enough for a grubstake -- but they were not so much interested in mining as they were in making money off of the miners through their business ventures. As Lancer looked down on the street below, he spotted Wyatt in his well-known black coat and hat. The thick, flowing handlebar mustache was Wyatt's other distinguishing feature, and was practically a trademark of the entire Earp clan.

Wyatt had made himself a reputation for taming wild towns. This morning he seemed a bit cautious as he walked along the wooden planks that made up Tombstone's sidewalks. He was headed to his office at an unusually early hour.

Lancer knew Wyatt had been uneasy lately. The Cowboy Gang and the latest to join them, Ike Clanton, were causing trouble. It was trouble of a petty sort, but it was making the Earp brothers uncomfortable. Lancer suspected a fight was coming but was hoping they would avoid it.

Could this be the dread Lancer felt in his soul? Was a battle about to happen? Suddenly a knock came at the door. He looked at his watch again. A half hour had passed seemingly in a moment. It was Javy with breakfast. Lancer meandered to the door, wondering where the time had gone. He could smell the freshly brewed coffee even before he reached for the doorknob.

"Morning, Señor Lancer. I have your breakfast just the way you like it," Javy said, moving through the open portal. "The coffee, she smells good, no?"

Lancer smiled. "Yes, Javy, it does. Is that chicory I smell?"

"It is, señor," the manservant said, grinning widely. "My wife, she wanted to surprise you."

His nose in the air, taking in the aroma, Lancer reached over and poured the hot liquid himself, not waiting for Javy to do the task.

"Ahhhh," Lancer said after the first sip. "Now that's mighty fine coffee. Brings back memories of New Orleans, it does."

Javy grinned even wider, knowing his wife had made the right decision.

"Give my regards to your woman, please. I know this was not an inexpensive choice."

"The chicory, she imported it all the way from New Orleans," Javy said. "But for you, Señor Lancer, she is always happy to make a sacrifice."

Lancer reached into his robe and pulled out the customary $20 gold piece to reward his manservant. He took out a second piece and started to offer it as well, but Javy refused. Lancer was taken aback.

"No, señor, one is enough. The other is a gift," Javy said firmly. "If I take the money, it would rob my wife of the gift she has given you, so I must decline."

Lancer understood. Javy was a proud man. Emilita, his wife, was even prouder. If she accepted the money, her sacrifice would be for naught. Lancer smiled and put his hand on Javy's shoulder.

"And we would not want to rob her of a blessing, now would we?"

A shake of the head told Lancer that Javy was in agreement. Javy suddenly broke the mellow mood by reaching into his pocket and pulling out a telegram.

"I almost forgot, this came for you this morning. I hope it is good news. But in your profession, I know it may not be."

Lancer took the telegram and saw it was a new assignment -- if he chose to take it.

"Lancer, please come to El Paso. I need your help. The matter is extremely urgent and needs your attention."

It was signed by Town Marshal Dallas Stoudenmire. He had gained a reputation for dealing with his adversaries quickly with a gun and not looking back. His reputation came largely from a fight in which he'd killed four men in just five seconds. The unkind part of those killings was that they included an innocent Mexican bystander and an unarmed drunk. The violence began over name-calling. That was how things seemed to go in the wild West -- minor transgressions ballooned into trouble, way out of proportion to the original harm done.

Lancer knew that if Dallas Stoudenmire was seeking his help, it must be something very important. Stoudenmire was not a man who would off-handedly ask for help from others. So this was a job Lancer was going to take, and take seriously.

He scribbled on a piece of paper, "On my way – Lancer."

"Javy, take my reply to the telegraph office and send it," he said. The servant took the paper and nodded. "I will be back to pack your bags in half an hour, señor."

Lancer sat down to begin his breakfast. He would leave town this very night. He'd stop by Virgil Earp's office first. Something bad was surely brewing, and Virgil perhaps had some inkling of what it was.

Jonah Rantz spotted Lancer coming downstairs and realized he had not prepared Lancer's morning drink. He quickly poured a coffee and a shot of whiskey. He knew the man in black would stop by the bar before heading out the door. Lancer was not always predictable, except when it came to such habits. Lancer understood that being too predictable in his line of work was a danger he could not afford.

"Thank you, Jonah," Lancer said, reaching for the coffee cup. "I always enjoy your being right on top of things."

"No worries, Lancer. I always appreciate a predictable customer," Jonah replied.

Lancer stopped in mid-sip and put the coffee down. He pushed it away as well as the whiskey. Rantz stood surprised for a moment. The look on Rantz's face told the story. He had offended the man he served each morning, or so he thought.

"Wipe that look off your face, Jonah," Lancer said with a sheepish smile. "I have offended myself."

Rantz was confused. He didn't know what the hired gun meant.

"You are exactly right. I have become predictable," Lancer pointed out. "It is a luxury I cannot afford. You see, if I follow a pattern, that leads to complacency. And the next time I lack the concentration of an inchworm, I might end up dead."

Rantz breathed a sigh of relief. He completely understood where Lancer was coming from. Lancer was well-liked but he had enemies, and enemies were something you could not afford in Tombstone. The town was rough, and doing the same thing over and over would lead those enemies into laying a trap. Lancer was not going to be trapped.

"So, should I not prepare the coffee and red-eye every morning as I have for so long?"

"No, you should not," Lancer said. "Starting tomorrow, or when I get back, we'll do something different. Maybe I'll have my morning beverages in my room or something. I'll figure it out."

Lancer quickly finished his coffee and downed the shot of whiskey. His face broke into a wide grin. "Starting tomorrow," he said, winking.

Rantz smiled back and took the two drinking vessels off the bar. Lancer reached into his pocket to pay the man but the barkeep held up his hand in refusal.

"You've paid with me with the kind of advice that I too needed to hear. My life also has become, shall we say, 'predictable.'"

Lancer's walk down the dusty Tombstone streets felt strange. He suspected that when he came back, Tombstone would not be the same. He could not put his finger on it, but there was just something odd in the air, and he didn't like this feeling at all.

Suddenly he came face to face with Roberta Glazer.

"Mr. Lancer, how nice to see you so early this fine morning." The raven-haired beauty smiled coquettishly at him while speaking in her smooth Southern drawl. "I am so looking forward to our meeting later this evening."

Lancer was momentarily transfixed. While trying to identify that strange feeling in the air, he had forgotten he was having drinks and maybe dinner with the lady merchant. Roberta Glazer, known to her friends as Robbie, ran the largest mercantile establishment in Tombstone. She sold nearly everyone in the town their dry goods, and had

begun an import business to carry some of the
foreign goods requested by Tombstone's growing
population of immigrants from Europe. She even
stocked Lancer's favorite exotic treat, Turkish
Delight.

"Robbie, why yes, of course. I'm sorry. I was a bit
preoccupied,"

"Not too preoccupied, I hope."

"No, no, of course not," Lancer assured her.

He was uncharacteristically nervous but quickly
regained his bearings. He mustn't let the lady see
him as weak. Although some women liked that
little-boy trait in men, Robbie Glazer was not one
of them. She played along, usually. But she liked
her men strong, which was why she was trying to
corral Lancer. His reputation for having never been
corralled only gave her more pleasure and
determination in the pursuit.

"I don't suppose you'd be interested in meeting
another night? I only say this because I will be
leaving for El Paso this evening. I've taken an
assignment there."

Her face fell. She was not happy to hear that a job
was taking precedence over her affection. "Of
course, Mr. Lancer," she said woodenly.

Lancer immediately detected her disappointment and decided to salvage the situation as best he could. "Let me offer a compromise," he said. "Let's say dinner at six, instead of drinks at eight and a late supper."

Robbie Glazer warmed up a bit and forced a grin.

"If that is what needs to be, then so be it," she said. "I'll get someone to cover the store so I can leave early. You do propose a problem, Mr. Lancer, but I know your work is important and since this may be the last chance we have to be together, I guess I can accommodate you."

The mention of "the last chance" didn't go down with Lancer as easily as she said it. He was going to El Paso for a dangerous job and he still had this uneasy feeling about whatever the future held for Tombstone. He leaned in and kissed Robbie on the cheek, doffed his hat and started to move on. He turned as he passed her. "Five o'clock, dinner in my room?"

She smiled a half-smile in silent agreement. Then he turned away and so did she. As she went on her way, a wide smile graced her face. Dinner in the man's room meant he might still be there in the morning. This was in her plan. Roberta Glazer never failed in her plans.

Lancer didn't bother to knock when he arrived at
Virgil Earp's door. He just walked in. His
friendship with the Earps was well known. Doc
Holliday, Virgil, Morgan and Wyatt were a team
he could work with and trust forever. They were
good men. They had their flaws, but this was the
West and who didn't? The Earps had come to
Tombstone not to be lawmen but to strike it rich
off the men who mined the silver, by operating a
stage line and other businesses. None of them
panned out. The women of the family blamed
Wyatt, and the only outlet the men were finding
was the law. At least it's what they told
themselves, and they were fairly good at it, at least
by reputation.

The room was filled with guns being readied as
Lancer walked in. "Morning, gentlemen," Lancer
said. "There's something brewing, I see. Or do my
eyes deceive me?"

"No time for small talk," Morgan said tersely, not
even looking up at Lancer.

"This I can see."

Wyatt cocked a shotgun and looked through the
sight, making sure he didn't point it at anyone in
the room. He put the gun down and finally looked
directly at Lancer.

"It's come," Wyatt said bluntly. The Clantons and the McLaurys had laid down the challenge and Billy Claiborne was joining them. They'd had enough of the Earps and Doc Holliday. They were ready for a showdown and the Earps were ready to give it to them.

Lancer went straight to the obvious. "Where and when?"

Virgil's answer was short and sharp. "Tomorrow."

"The O.K. Corral," Wyatt added.

Lancer knew what was coming. He also knew the Earps were not going to lose even if they had to break the law to get it done. Sheriff Johnny Behan would try to stop the showdown. Behan was a weak lawman, and since it was pretty much accepted he was on the take from the Cowboy gang, the Earp clan was not about to trust the sheriff. Wyatt had another reason for disliking Behan. The sheriff was a suitor to the woman Wyatt himself was after, Josephine Marcus.

"Make sure it's legal," Lancer warned.

"If they are carrying guns, it will be legal," Morgan said grimly. "You know the law -- no guns in the city limits."

Lancer was not impressed by that answer. He knew the law Morgan mentioned. In fact, he knew a lot about laws in general and had often considered going into lawyering. But he'd decided it wasn't his best skill, although most people who knew him said he would make an excellent lawyer.

"You know what I mean, Morg."

"Don't worry, it will be legal, my friend, it will be legal," Wyatt shot back. "We'll give them every opportunity to disarm."

"You know they won't. Not Ike, not Billy and certainly not the McLaury brothers," Lancer said. "They're way too proud."

"Pride can get you killed. You want to be a part of it?" This time it was Virgil's booming voice that offered up a prediction of what was to come.

Lancer knew deep-down it was going to end badly for someone. It was just a question of who. He also knew this was the reason for the jittery feeling he'd had since he woke up. And he wanted no part of it. What was about to come down was going to be bloody. Reputations would be soiled. Men would lie dead in the street. There was no way to stop it -- this was going to be history. And it was not his fight. He had another mission.

"No, I'll be on my way to El Paso. Got an assignment."

"Stoudenmire?" Virgil asked, raising his eyebrows.

"Old four-dead-in-five-seconds Stoudenmire?" Morgan chimed in. "What's he want with you?"

"Don't rightly know," Lancer answered truthfully.

Wyatt shrugged. "Well, if old Dallas is asking for your help, he needs you more than we do. You be careful down there, and we'll see you when you get back."

Lancer forced a sad smile that said to his friend, *You need to make damn sure you get through this next day.* Lancer didn't like losing friends. Wyatt caught the look on Lancer's face and nodded. They knew each other well enough to read each other's thoughts.

"What about Doc, Ringo, Curly Bill?" Lancer inquired about the other players who made Tombstone a dangerous place.

"Doc's sickly again," Virgil said, shrugging. "Maybe if he's well enough."

"We could sure use the extra hand," Wyatt pointed out, looking through the sights of another rifle. "Haven't heard from Bill and Ringo. Chances are those cowards are holding back, waiting for the dust to clear."

Lancer headed for the door but turned when he reached it.

"I won't put it past them," he said, looking straight at the brothers. "Watch your backs."

Lancer closed the door behind him and stood gazing at the main street in front of him. He looked right and left, then headed to the livery to see how Lincoln was doing. The great black horse needed to be ready for the long ride to El Paso. Lancer thought about postponing his trip a day, going back in and offering his services to the Earp brothers. Looking up at the morning sun, he thought better of it. The premonition he'd had did not include him. His journey was taking him to Texas on the Mexican border. He hoped he'd return to find his friends still alive. He had a feeling they were going to come out okay at the O.K.

It was 4:45 and Lancer sat in the parlor of the hotel, waiting for the woman he'd sup with this night. The book in his hands detailed the latest in the longstanding legacy of Abraham Lincoln. He loved the man, perhaps more than his own father. Lincoln was the father figure of a nation to him. Yes, George Washington was the recognized father of the country and rightfully so, but birthing a nation was probably easier than fighting to keep it from ripping itself apart. Lincoln didn't live long enough to see his legacy take hold.

The voice of Doc Holliday interrupted his thoughts. "I do declare, Mr. Lancer, is that a book on that scoundrel Lincoln you are reading?"

"I guess it takes one to know one, right Doctor Holliday?"

Holliday laughed out loud at the suggestion.

"You are correct in your assumption, Lancer, and it is because of that very distinct impression it gives people, I no longer use the full term 'Doctor,' preferring the abbreviated version in its obscurity."

"You do have a way with words, Doc," Lancer said, putting the book down. "Won't you sit?"

Holliday took the opportunity and sat across from Lancer. He picked up the book and quickly put it down as the cough from his consumption overtook him.

"I am sorry. This continues to get me down," Holliday said, coming out of the cough and holding his kerchief away from his mouth. "It will be the death of me, I fear."

Lancer did not comment. Everyone knew Doc was living day-to-day, and his drinking was not helping.

"Where did you get this unkindly publication, sir?"

"It is by an unknown author," Lancer began. "I believe it's a soldier who happened to be on the detail hunting for Booth."

"Another scoundrel indeed," Doc said disdainfully. "There is no honor in assassination. No matter how much harm a man does in his life, everyone should have the opportunity to face his accuser, even if it is to the death. A duel might have been better suggested."

Doc grinned before coughing again and summoning the waiter to bring him a drink.

"Have you heard of what is on the morrow?"

Lancer sat up straighter and looked Doc directly in the eye. "Will you participate?"

Doc leaned closer to the man who asked the question and looked *him* directly in the eye.

"I have every intention," he said before downing his whiskey in one gulp. "And your intentions?"

Before Lancer could answer, Roberta Glazer came up from behind and put her hand on Lancer's shoulder. Doc looked up and grinned again. "And there are no further questions needed," he said as he got up. "Enjoy your night, both of you. I know I would."

With that, Doc Holliday headed toward the gaming tables where he would be joined by Big Nose Kate. Together they would try to best the gamblers. Lancer was hoping it would be a short night for Doc. He'd have to be at his best with Wyatt in the morning. It would be four against five and someone was going to get killed. Lancer hoped his friends would not be lying in Boot Hill upon his return.

He knew this was going to be a short night for himself. Dinner for sure, maybe more, but he was leaving for El Paso tonight. He did not want to be tempted to end up at the O.K. Corral tomorrow. Something told him it was not his place to be.

CHAPTER TWO

Javy Lopez made his way up the stairway of the hotel on his way to Lancer's room. He had taken care of Lincoln, packed Lancer's bags, and stuffed the saddlebags with the usual complement of food, hardtack and of course the Turkish Delight Lancer always carried with him on long trips. Javy had heard about the coming fight and was wondering if maybe his boss's plans had changed. He didn't think Lancer would abandon his friends, but at the same time he knew the man had loyalties to his duties.

It wouldn't take long for Javy to get an answer.

As Javy approached Lancer's room, the door opened suddenly. There stood Roberta Glazer, dressed in the clothes she came with. She was smiling, although Javy noticed her hair was somewhat mussed. Lancer was at the door, ushering his guest out. He looked confident. Her smile had a glow.

"Javy, right on time," Lancer said.

"Miss Glazer," Javy greeted the woman.

She nodded, then turned and gave Lancer a small but daringly passionate kiss on the lips.

"You take care," she told Lancer. "I won't accept the postponement of another dinner, darling."

Lancer held her tightly for a moment, then lightly kissed her forehead. His failure to reciprocate her fervent kiss brought a pout to her lips.

"You are a scoundrel, Mr. Lancer," she said. "But I do so love a challenge."

Robbie smiled again, moving to the end of the hall before turning and blowing him a kiss. He snatched it out of the air and put it in his pocket close to his heart. Then she was gone. Javy moved into the room and began the final preparations for Lancer's departure.

"Will you still be leaving tonight?" Javy asked.

"I will," came the reply. "Believe it or not, I am fully rested and comfortable with starting the trip this evening rather than tomorrow morning."

His manservant glanced around the room to make sure everything was in order. Javy knew Lancer was confident but he understood, too, that Lancer wanted to be there to support the Earp clan. Realizing the fight was not something Lancer wished to be part of, Javy would say nothing else.

Lancer could tell that Javy had an opinion on this. "You think I'm making a mistake," he said.

"It is not for me to say, señor."

"I know, Javy, but I want you to say."

Javy Lopez had known Lancer for a decade, and not once had Lancer spoken to him in this way. Javy wasn't sure how to approach it.

"Permission to speak freely?"

Lancer nodded, knowing the answer would come from the heart of a man he trusted.

"A man looks at his friends and questions whether they are doing the right thing. He must put his trust in his soul. If he feels his friends are doing right, he must let them play out their hand. If he feels they are doing wrong, he must attempt to stop them. Under no circumstances, however, must he interfere, especially if he feels what his friends are about to do does not involve his destiny – just theirs."

Lancer put his hand to his chin and walked around the room. He had not expected such a philosophical answer from Javy Lopez. He grinned and reached for the brandy sitting on the small table. He poured two drinks and handed one to his servant.

"Aristotle could not have said it better, my friend," Lancer said, raising a glass. "Shall we toast good friends and friendships?"

Javy awkwardly accepted the drink and joined in the toast.

"I don't know who this Astritottle is, señor, but I hope he's a smarter man than me."

Lancer downed his drink and put his hand on Javy's shoulder.

"He was a great man," Lancer said. "But not as great as the friend you are to me."

It was time to begin the long ride to El Paso. Lancer grabbed his hat and coat and gun as Javy followed behind him with the small bag carrying Lancer's other gear.

The trip from Tombstone to El Paso would be 300 miles. At a pace of 50 miles a day, an aggressive one, Lancer would be there in a week. There were a few towns along the way to restock supplies, but it was still a lonely and somewhat treacherous stretch. Bandits frequented the trails, coming up from Mexico, hitting locals and heading back before the sparse U.S. lawmen could block their escape. The Texas Rangers would be the best of the best, but not until he got across the New Mexico Territory, which took up most of the ride.

Lancer headed out of Tombstone and didn't look back. He didn't want one more temptation in his mind. Javy was right. It was not his fight to get into. Lancer had a strange peace about him despite his worry over his friends. A half mile out of town, he saw two figures on horses coming his way. It wasn't long before he would come upon the McLaury brothers heading into Tombstone.

Coming face to face with the pair, they pulled to a halt on the roadway. They must have known he knew about the coming fight. Lancer wasn't about to give up what he knew.

"Lancer," Tom McLaury stiffly greeted the man opposite him.

"Tom, Frank," came the reply.

"Going somewhere?" Frank asked.

Lancer nodded. "Heading toward your place, actually."

"What business have you in McNeal?" Tom asked, raising an eyebrow.

"None. Just gonna bed down for the night," Lancer said. "Moving on to El Paso in the morning. Hope to make it to McNeal in a few hours."

The brothers felt uncomfortable, despite knowing Lancer would not be a part of what was to come. Still, they were not convinced.

Frank decided to test him. "You know what's coming?"

"I do," Lancer said sternly. "Not my fight. But if you are going up against the Earps, you will have your hands full. They won't need me."

Both men chafed in their saddles.

"Still, much obliged you won't be partaking," Tom finally said.

Lancer doffed his hat and started to move on. As he passed, Tom McLaury raised his voice.

"When you get there, eat at Millie Down's Place," he said. "Best darned food east of Tombstone. Tell Millie I sent you."

"I'll do exactly that," Lancer promised.

"Tom's sweet on her, so take it with a grain," Frank yelled, laughing as he did.

Tom took off his hat and slapped his brother across the chest playfully. There was a lack of confidence in their conversation. It said this may be the last time the three men would ever speak. History was about to happen.

As he approached the outskirts of McNeal in the Arizona Territory, Lancer couldn't help but think about the conversation he'd had a few hours earlier. It was a small town, and Millie Down's Place wasn't hard to find. Lancer knew the McLaurys had a spread not far from there. The only rooms to be had were next door to the restaurant, and while it was past midnight, there was a lighted candle in the rooming house window. It suggested to Lancer the proprietor was probably still awake.

Lancer tied up Lincoln and walked in. He didn't see anyone and was about to ring the bell when he saw a note attached to it.

"If you need a room, take a room key from behind the desk. I will collect in the morning and Don't disturb the other guests. P.S. Leave your horse in front. Ain't no one gonna steal a horse in this town after 10 o'clock."

Lancer smiled, selected Room Key No. 4 and headed up the stairs. Number Four was clean enough and all he wanted was a soft place to rest his weary body. Moments later he was off to sleep.

The morning sunshine came soon enough, peeking through the curtain-less window. Lancer noticed a wash basin on the wooden dresser. The water pitcher was full and the water was fresh. He was ready to start a new day.

Lancer thought to himself about what was going to happen in Tombstone this morning and wondered if there was any news to speak of. He grabbed his gear and headed down the steps to greet the morning. A man stood behind the desk at the entrance and looked up as Lancer approached.

"Came in late last night and saw the note," Lancer said. "Stayed in Room 4. How much do I owe you?"

"Four bits," was the answer. "You staying a second night?"

Lancer shook his head.

"Passing through," he said as he counted out the change. "Any news from Tombstone this morning?"

The clerk shook his head.

"Epitaph don't come out until later in the day," he said. "You expecting something?"

Lancer didn't answer but headed to the door and over to Millie Down's. It was a bright day in McNeal, and while he was anxious about news from Tombstone, he knew good news travels slowly, bad news travels fast. Word had not yet arrived in the McLaurys' hometown, so he was confident in waiting.

Millie Down's Place was crowded. Cowboys, ranch hands and local businessmen had a fondness for Millie's cooking. It wasn't she who did the actual cooking, but her mother. Millie had a head for numbers and her mother had a knack for using frying pans. The combination made it the most profitable business in town.

"Right over there is a table, mister." Millie pointed to a corner table as she approached Lancer. "No need for a menu. All we got today is our special, ham and eggs, biscuits and coffee. Be with you in a minute."

A few people noticed the man in black as he moved to his table. One or two may have recognized him, but most just went about their business. To those who did notice, it was more like "who is this stranger in town." The town sheriff looked up from his eggs long enough to stare for a moment at Lancer and then at Lancer's gun. He must have noticed the crossed lances on the holster because he stared for a long time at that particular spot before going back to his breakfast. He sipped his coffee and suddenly got up, walking over to Lancer's table.

"Mr. Lancer, I presume?"

"Yes, and you are Sheriff--?"

"Henry Major. Sheriff Henry Major," the man said matter-of-factly.

Lancer reached out to shake hands but the sheriff didn't take up the offer. "Friend of the Earps, aren't you?"

Lancer continued to hold out his hand in greeting until the sheriff finally returned a tepid shake.

"Is it against the law to have such friends?"

The sheriff frowned and raised his voice. "Maybe not, but we don't take much stock in folks who curry favor with scum." The chatter at surrounding tables instantly fell off.

The tense silence in the air was suddenly and politely interrupted when Millie appeared out of nowhere. Her smiling face and calm demeanor brought a fast end to the imminent ruckus, to everyone's relief.

"Oh now Henry," she playfully chastised the sheriff, "you go back to your table and eat your breakfast. I won't stand for my guests being disturbed by talk of gunmen and gunfights. Hush up and leave this man alone."

The sheriff stood his ground for a moment but knew he had no right to go any further so he silently returned to his table. Millie drew in closer to Lancer, pretending to brush crumbs off the table as she leaned in to whisper.

"There's trouble brewing and everyone in town is edgy. "Sorry you had to be his target this morning. I'll get your breakfast, ah, Mr. Lancer is it?"

"Just Lancer," he replied. "Tom McLaury said you served the best meals east of Tombstone, so here I am."

Millie stopped what she was doing and became more cautious. "You know Tom?"

"Only somewhat. Passed him along the road on the way here. He was heading to Tombstone."

Millie perked up quickly, very worried.

"Did he say anything to you, I mean, about what was going on?"

"No, but his brother said he was sweet on you," Lancer said, smiling. "And I can see why, Miss Millie."

Millie blushed but caught herself quickly and moved back to the kitchen.

Lancer wanted to hear as much as anyone about what was happening in Tombstone. However, right now he was hungry and the smell of ham and eggs, and fresh biscuits overpowered his thoughts. It wasn't long before Millie came back with a large plate loaded with a steaming hot breakfast.

"Three eggs, a slab of ham, a pair of biscuits and black coffee," Millie said, placing the plate on the table. "Did I miss anything?"

"No, I think you got it all."

Most of the diners had finished their meals and left the diner. The sheriff was gone, too. Millie sat down across from Lancer. She seemed to have something on her mind.

"May I ask you a question?" she began hesitantly.

Lancer half-smiled and nodded as he buttered a biscuit.

"Do you think I'll ever see Tom again?" she asked bluntly. "I mean we're not spoken for, but you know, a girl has a right to expect certain things, and well, I guess I'm kinda sweet on him too."

Lancer paused and thought carefully before answering. He knew the Earps were not a forgiving group. He loved Wyatt and the brothers, but they were a family first and lawmen second. Anyone who got between them didn't stand much of a chance. The McLaurys were not gunfighters. They were ranchers and perhaps rustlers, but the gunplay honors went to Johnny Ringo and Curly Bill. Lancer knew if Tom and Frank tangled with Wyatt and Doc, chances were good they would not be returning to McNeal. At least not standing up.

"Well, Miss Down, I don't know exactly what is going to happen in Tombstone. But one thing I've learned, when there is a dispute, the worst way to settle it is with gunplay," he said, leaning over to take her hand in his. "Maybe cooler heads will prevail and you'll be fixing supper tonight right here for Tom and Frank."

Millie felt relieved but only for a moment. She knew from his talk and walk that Lancer was an educated man, and educated men didn't make things worse for womenfolk -- they tried to make things better, even if "better" meant telling a lie. She patted Lancer's hand to signal the end of the conversation, and with a tear in her eye she dismissed herself. Lancer suddenly didn't feel much like eating. He sat for a minute and sipped his coffee, trying to get his appetite back. He ate half the breakfast, but not before an older woman approached him.

Wearing an apron, with the smell of ham and eggs on her clothes, she was obviously Millie's mother.

"Mr. Lancer, you should finish your breakfast and leave town," she said in a low voice. "There are some men who are friends with Tom and Frank, and well, they think you are friends of the Earps. You probably should leave before they get riled up. Especially if word comes that the boys didn't fare too well in Tombstone."

Lancer knew he was getting good advice. He took a couple more quick bites before getting up.

"Oh, and by the way, Mr. Lancer," the woman continued quietly, "thank you for trying to ease Millie's fears. Truth is, Tom McLaury is a law-breaking criminal who doesn't deserve my Millie. Just between us, you understand."

With a nod and a tip of the hat, Lancer reached into his pocket for his money. The woman waved him off to indicate it was on the house. He smiled his thanks and headed out the door.

Lancer could feel Sheriff Major's eyes glued to him from across the street. Several men wearing guns were watching too. Without being obvious about it, Lancer surveyed the street, trying to get a bead on who might draw on him first.

A man in his forties looked like the most plausible candidate. Lancer stood at Lincoln's side as the stranger came closer. Lancer made sure he didn't make any sudden moves, but his eyes continued to roam and keep track of the others. He was confident he could take out the gunman but wasn't sure who might step up in the man's defense once he did.

"You like licking Wyatt Earp's boots, mister?" the man sneered, coming to a sudden stop that blocked Lincoln's path.

"I don't want to fight you, sir. I'm getting on my horse and moving on," Lancer replied. "So if you will step aside, I'll be on my way."

The words enraged the stranger. "I don't step aside for no man, especially a friend of the scum of the earth from Tombstone."

Lancer moved away from Lincoln and prepared to defend himself.

"Look, mister, I call a lot of people friends," Lancer said. "Maybe I'll even call you friend one day. That is, if you live that long."

The last words were too much for the gunman. As he drew, Lancer puller his gun first and put a deadly shot right into the man's heart. The stranger never even cleared leather. As he collapsed on the ground, Lancer held his gun out, looking to see who would challenge him next.

The booming voice of Sheriff Major came from the sidewalk opposite the dead man. "You've made your point, Lancer. Move on. It was self-defense and everyone saw it happen. Now get out of my town."

Lancer cautiously holstered his weapon, mounted Lincoln and walked the great horse slowly out of town. As he did, he continued to look at every building along the way. He saw a window on the second story open and assumed a rifle was coming next. But it was the top of a dress of a dance hall girl, who was peeking out to see what the noise was all about. Lancer sighed and Lincoln's pace picked up just enough to avoid any more challenges in McNeal.

CHAPTER THREE

Dallas Stoudenmire was an old man by law
enforcement standards, but at age 35 he ruled El
Paso with an iron fist. It was rare for him not to
stand and deliver when the bad guys rolled up on
someone not so deserving of their trouble. He
stood well over six feet tall and had always looked
older than his age. He had enlisted in the Army at
age 15, but his underage status was soon
discovered and he was discharged from the Army
of the South in Alabama. The problem was, he
wasn't prone to giving up and he kept getting
taller. As the War Between the States progressed,
he reached 6'4" and signed on legally with the
Alabama 45th. Twice wounded, he would carry the
shell fragments in him for the rest of his life.

After the war, he moved out West and spent
several years as a Texas Ranger. A sharp dresser,
he would rival Wyatt Earp and Doc Holliday if
their paths had ever crossed. Like Lancer, he was a
hit with the ladies, and despite being less educated
and having a quicker temper when he drank, he
was mostly a gentleman. Unlike the man he
summoned from Tombstone, he wore a two-gun
rig.

Stoudenmire had been the marshal in the border
town for less than six months when his troubles
mounted to the point of needing the help of an

outsider. Still considered an outsider himself, Stoudenmire wanted a second opinion, if not a second gun.

The Manning family had been in El Paso for decades and was involved in many unsavory activities. But the clan was prosperous and well-liked. Most of the locals called them friends. While Stoudenmire did a good job of cleaning up El Paso, he was still the new guy in town and often clashed with the Mannings. His brother-in-law, Doc Cummings, had convinced him to take the job, and his wife, Isabella, liked the idea of living close to Mexico.

The Mannings were getting anxious because Stoudenmire was causing them problems. Despite their friends in the community, folks in the capitol were starting to look at El Paso with a new eye. The city had always been considered a bastard child -- more New Mexico than Texas. But in the capitol, El Paso was viewed as a key to the future of Texas. Its closeness to the border meant more commerce, and more commerce meant more money in state coffers.

Doc Cummings was coming out of the local saloon one night, having had too much to drink. In his path was James Manning. Manning saw Doc coming his way and neither man was about to step aside for the other.

"Move it on over," Cummings declared as he spotted Manning.

"You ain't your brother-in-law and you ain't moving me out the way," Manning growled. "Now step aside."

Suddenly Bill Parsons stepped out of a doorway and found himself between the two men. He immediately sensed the tension in the air and knew he had bumbled into the wrong place at the wrong time.

"Now, are you not one of his friends?" Doc asked Parson unsteadily while pointing at Manning.

"I'm not getting in the middle of this!" Parsons squealed in fright. "Please, let me pass by."

As Parsons tried to get out of the way, Doc grabbed him by the arm and spun him back between the two men. Parsons fell back onto a bench in front of the saloon, and Manning reached to steady him. Out of the corner of his eye, he saw Doc reaching too. Fearing Doc was going for his weapon, Manning pulled his first.

A shot rang out and Doc stood motionless for a moment. As the crowd came running out of the saloon, Cummings crumpled into the street, bleeding profusely.

"What have you done? What have you ---?" Doc's voice trailed off as he passed into eternity.

Manning stood holding his weapon at his side, still smoking.

"You killed Doc Cummings!" Parson shouted, still on the bench where he had fallen. "You killed him!"

The crowd gathered around Manning.

"I had to! He pulled first! It was self-defense, I swear it was self-defense!" Manning pleaded.

Stoudenmire came running down the street, a shotgun in his hands. Manning stood over the body of Doc Cummings.

"Drop it, Jim!" Stoudenmire ordered, leveling his shotgun at Manning's chest.

"He pulled first. Honest, he pulled first," Manny protested, lowering his handgun.

"I'll take that," Stoudenmire barked. "As for the cause, it's for a judge to decide."

Manning stared angrily at the lawman. He was sure he was in the right but he knew Stoudenmire wouldn't hesitate to kill him right then and there. Manning had just killed Isabella's brother, and all the marshal needed was an inch before taking Manning's life.

"Go tell my brothers," Manning ordered Parsons. "Tell them what happened."

Parsons looked over at the marshal, who nodded in assent. Stoudenmire knew what was coming and he knew he needed to be prepared. Better to be prepared for what you know than what you guess, he thought. Parsons headed for the Manning Ranch while Stoudenmire marched James Manning over to the jail. It was going to be a long night, The marshal turned to the barkeep standing with his arms crossed on the steps above the street.

"Send over some grub and lots of coffee, will ya Charlie? Lots of coffee."

Charlie Dankens gave a thumbs up to the marshal and headed back inside to prepare the food. No one was going to get any sleep this night.

It was a quiet jailhouse with no inmates at the moment, save the new one. James Manning entered the cell without a word. He knew nothing would happen quickly. It was an hour ride to the Manning Ranch and an hour back. His brothers, Frank and Jeff, would be returning heavily armed to confront the marshal. Stoudenmire was not about to let his prisoner go. James Manning was going to stand trial for murder. If a court acquitted him, which it probably would in this town, Marshal Stoudenmire might just have to take matters into his own hands.

Parsons rode as fast as he could to the Manning Ranch, reaching it in record time on a horse that was on the brink of exhaustion when they got there. Jeff Manning heard the rider coming and went outside. His brother Frank had gone to bed early.

"Jeff, Frank! Come quick!" Parsons yelled as he raced to the front of the house.

Jeff, knowing something was wrong, ran over to meet Parsons.

"What's the fuss all about?"

"It's James -- he's in jail!" Parsons sputtered, nearly out of breath. "Stoudenmire took him in."

Frank had come to the door half asleep but now was wide awake. "For what? What's he supposed to have done?"

"Murder!"

The word struck Frank and Jeff speechless. They looked at each other and then back at Parsons for more details.

"Doc Cummings!" Parsons blurted out.

The two brothers knew this was about as serious as it gets. Even if James were innocent, there would be a fight. Frank headed back inside looking for his handgun. Jeff started to follow but Parsons grabbed his arm.

"It was self-defense. I saw it. I was there and I was the only one who was there," Parsons explained hurriedly. "I swear, the marshal will have to believe me."

"Right, believe you," was all Jeff could mutter.

Jeff raced inside where Frank was loading his pistol and grabbing a rifle to go along with it. Jeff put his hand on Frank's arm, stopping it in mid-air.

"Look, maybe Parsons is right," Jeff said. "If he did see it and it was self-defense, Stoudenmire would have to let James go."

"Cummings was family. Would you let it go if someone killed me, even if it was justified?"

Jeff thought about that for a moment and realized his brother was right. Stoudenmire and the Mannings had been feuding since the day the marshal was hired in El Paso. This gave him purpose and reason, even if it were a justified killing. Jeff decided to follow Frank's lead. Bullets were made for guns and guns were made for killing. He began loading his gun. This was going to be a long night.

Leaving McNeal and the town friendly to the McLaurys behind, Lancer moved on toward El Paso. He hoped to make it to Hachita in a couple of days. The weather was good, which was in his favor, but the trail was still filled with Indians, Mexican bandits and cattle rustlers who moved with ease back and forth across the border. New Mexico Territory, like its Arizona counterpart, was wide and wild, with few federal troops to keep order.

Fifteen miles out of Hachita, Lincoln crested a hill and stopped cold. The great horse had sensed something wasn't right, and Lancer knew when that happened, he'd best pay heed. The sound of voices drifted up from the valley a hundred yards below. Lancer could hear anger in the words, carried by the wind. He moved Lincoln behind some rocks and dismounted. He couldn't make out exactly what was being said, but his U.S. Army binoculars helped him understand what was going on below.

The round cap on the rear portion of one man's head gave away much of what was taking place. He was a rabbi, and his horse and cart revealed even more information on his plight. There wasn't much for the man of his Jewish God to do when confronted by four men of dubious reputation. The laughter coming from down below at the rabbi's expense told Lancer this was an unfair confrontation. If there was one thing he hated most in the world, it was lack of fairness.

He could see one man going through the rabbi's cart. The man started throwing clothes into the air. When the tools of the rabbi's trade were tossed onto the ground, Lancer decided it was time to intervene. He knew enough about the Jewish culture to understand the sacred things the rabbi was carrying were extremely personal. A menorah ended up on the ground, thrown hard as if in an attempt to break it.

Lancer mounted Lincoln and moved cautiously ahead. He didn't make a hard charge, choosing instead not to startle the men. About 30 yards away, one of them noticed him. A rifle was pointed toward Lancer but he kept coming.

"This is a private affair, mister. No concern of yours," the man with the rifle shouted.

Lancer didn't stop. As he got to the spot where the group was harassing the rabbi, he leaned in and spoke calmly.

"No worries. Ain't none of my affair. Still, harassing a man of God might get you a couple weeks in hell, if you get my drift."

One of the other men didn't hide his surprise at hearing this. "Man of God? You mean he's a priest or something?"

"A rabbi. A Jewish priest you might say," Lancer shot back. "That candelabra you tossed on the ground is a menorah. Used to highlight the miracle of the Maccabees. Jewish people light it during Hanukkah."

The man with the rifle began to laugh.

"Hanawhat?"

"Hanukkah," the rabbi corrected him. "The Festival of Lights."

The man heading up the group turned quickly to the rabbi and spoke sternly. "Shut up and give us your watch and whatever else you got in there of value!" He turned to Lancer. "And you, mister, like we said, this ain't none of your affair."

At that point the rabbi's dog barked at the lead man, who pulled out his handgun and started to take aim at the pooch. Lightning fast, Lancer pulled his own gun and fired. The bullet knocked the weapon out of the man's hand. Lancer then positioned himself to shoot to kill the man in charge.

"I'm making it my affair," Lancer announced as the gang froze. "Rabbi, gather your things and move on down the road. I'll hold these men here until you're safely away."

The horses stirred and the lead man retorted, "You think you can hold off the four of us?"

One of the robbers glanced at Lancer's holster and noticed the crossed lances."

"Dennis, look," he said quietly to the man in charge. Dennis now realized he was facing the famous Lancer.

"Sorry, Mr. Lancer, I didn't know it was you," Dennis said meekly. "We were just having some fun and didn't mean to do any harm to the priest. You can go on about your business and we'll head to Tombstone, okay?"

Keeping his gun pointed at the gang, Lancer nodded. "You heard any news out of Tombstone?" he asked.

Dennis was the first to speak up. "Heard there was a big gunfight. A couple cowboys dead, but not sure who did what. Might be some news in Hachita, if that is where you are headed. That's where I heard it, but that was yesterday so there may be more news by now."

"Much obliged," Lancer said, keeping his gun on the group. "Now move out."

Lancer watched them go up over a hill before turning around and heading toward Hachita. It didn't take him long to catch up with the rabbi.

"I want to thank you, mister, but I don't even know your name," the rabbi said.

"It's Lancer and it's not necessary, Rabbi--?"

"Vinburg, Rabbi Joseph Vinburg, at your service," came the reply. "And you, do you have a first name?"

"Just Lancer."

"Well, Mr. Just Lancer, thank you again," Rabbi Vinburg said. "Will you share supper with me? And some very nice wine?"

Lancer nodded, this time with a smile. They rode together for a few miles, chatting until night started to fall and a place for supper looked right.

As Lancer gathered wood for the fire, Rabbi Vinburg set about the task of getting food from his cart. He had recently purchased carrots, beans and onions, which would make a fine stew. He was peeling the onions when he heard a gunshot that sounded close-by. The 45-year-old man of God jumped to his feet, looking around and hoping Lancer was the shooter and not the victim. Within moments his fears were put to rest.

Lancer came out of the bushes, holding a plump rabbit by the ears. "Sorry about the suddenness of my display of weaponry," he told his dinner companion, "but rabbits move more quickly than humans, and when you must act, you must act. This'll make a right fine addition to your stew."

The rabbi could only stare for a moment at the creature Lancer held by its ears.

The stare finally caught up with Lancer, who remembered his Old Testament.

"Leviticus," he stated. "Moses said it was unclean to eat a rabbit. Rabbi, I am sorry. I forgot in my haste."

The rabbi thought for a moment before speaking.

"It's all right. I'm not that Orthodox," he said with a smile. "You shot it, you skin it!"

Lancer shrugged his shoulders and let out a hearty laugh. He liked this holy man.

The night was warm. As they settled down to rabbit stew with beans and biscuits on the side, Lancer looked over inquisitively.

"There is an unnatural taste in the stew, if you don't mind me saying so," he said. "I'm not sure exactly what it is, but there seems to be a bit of spirits in it."

Reaching for a wooden box nearby, the rabbi pulled out a bottle. He grinned as he raised it to Lancer.

"It's kosher by all means, and now maybe the rabbit is too. Would you like a glass of it to go along with the creature?"

Lancer reached into his saddlebag and pulled out his own bottle.

"Thank you, but I prefer this. A nice Napoleon brandy always goes down better for me after a fine meal and before the sweet tooth takes hold."

Rabbi Vinburg raised a questioning eyebrow at mention of a sweet tooth. Lancer took that as an opportunity to bring out his favorite treat. He lifted a small box from the saddlebag and the aroma of

Turkish Delight promptly scented the air. It turned out the rabbi was no stranger to this sweet delicacy.

"Ah, Mr. Lancer, you are full of surprises," he said as he lifted a piece from the box. "I got hooked on this upon my first and only visit to Jerusalem."

"You have been there?"

"I had to go because, in my mind, if you are going to teach the word of God, you must first visit where it was delivered," the rabbi said. Then he caught himself. "I have not actually been to the mountain Moses carried the tablets from. I wanted to go, but circumstances kept me away from the desert. And you, I believe you are a man of the world as well."

Lancer knew his past was being sought, and for the first time in a long time, he felt like it was a good thing to share. He began telling the story of his life to this stranger who had now become his friend.

"My family was well-heeled, you might say, and my father's business interests took him to the Crimea and beyond. I was fortunate enough to go with him," Lancer said. "China, Japan and even a trip to India were part of where I spent my youth."

He explained his road to Jerusalem went through Cairo and he was amazed by the size of the pyramids. Once in the Holy City, he was able to take in the great sights most of his classmates would only read about. By the time Lancer got to the Civil War and his youthful battlefield commission, he was interrupted by the rabbi's snoring. He had put the man to sleep.

"And this is the real reason why I leave well enough alone when it comes to my early life," Lancer said with a wry smile and a low voice so as not to wake the man. "At least you could have waited until the good parts."

Lancer rolled over, covered himself with his blanket and went to sleep. Tomorrow he would be in Hachita in the New Mexico Territory. As he closed his eyes, his thoughts drifted to Tombstone. His hope was that there would be good news in Hachita and not news of a grave to be dug under the name "Wyatt Earp."

CHAPTER FOUR

The Manning brothers rode into El Paso while the town was buzzing with news of Doc Cummings' death. They didn't ride right up to the marshal's office, choosing instead to stop by the saloon and gather what information they could. They had Parsons' viewpoint and he'd be along shortly. His long ride had tuckered out his horse, and rather than take one of the Mannings' breed, he chose to cool down his own and arrive in town after they did.

The lively music and chatter in the Border Saloon stopped immediately when Frank Manning strode through the swinging doors. He was a man who commanded a presence, and after what had happened a few hours earlier, everyone had expected his arrival. And everyone in the place knew what was on his mind.

Manning walked slowly up to the bar, where the bartender had a drink waiting for him. Without hesitating, Manning swallowed the shot and clapped the glass down on the bar. Then he turned and addressed the crowd that was staring silently at him.

"Now all I know is what Parsons told me -- it was self-defense, Doc pulled first and then Stoudenmire took my brother into custody."

Manning surveyed the room. "Anyone here telling it different?"

The crowd remained silent, and that told Manning he had friends. Or, at least no one who would mess with him was in that bar at the moment.

"Good. Then who's with me?"

Half a dozen men lined up behind Manning and followed him through the swinging doors. Once outside, Jeff Manning fell in beside his brother and they marched across town to the jail. The anger welling up inside the two brothers was visible on their faces. They felt emboldened by the crowd at their back.

At the jailhouse, Marshal Dallas Stoudenmire waited with a shotgun loaded for bear. He'd not had time to go home to tell Isabella her brother was dead. He didn't know if he'd ever have the chance, because he knew the Mannings would come gunning for him. He saw them in the distance as they marched with a pair of torches to light the way.

"Marshal, send my brother out or we're coming in to get him!" Frank Manning shouted when the crowd arrived outside the jail.

Stoudenmire didn't hesitate to walk out the door with his shotgun leveled at the mob. He stood there for what seemed like an eternity.

"Let my brother go, and let him go now!" Frank ordered. "Everyone here saw it. Everyone knows Doc pulled first. Now if you want a fight, you'll get one."

The lawman stood his ground and addressed his comments to everyone.

"Now I'm not going to tell you someone is going to die before you get past me and get to James. And I'm not going to tell you I'll get two or three of you before you get me, and the dead may not even be the Mannings. But I will tell you right here and now to go home. When Judge Blakemore arrives in two days, you can all have your say, and I believe there won't be any gallows play here. Just remember the law is the law, and I ain't putting up with any vigilante justice."

His speech had its intended effect on the crowd. No one moved or said anything.

"You mean that, Marshal?" a lone voice finally called out.

"As sure as I'm holding this shotgun right here," he answered. "Now go home and let the law take its course. And that means you too, Manning. And let my wife sorrow in peace. Doc was her brother."

The crowd began to drift away and the Mannings knew they were beaten that night. Jeff started to pull his gun. Stoudenmire saw that and aimed his shotgun directly at Jeff's chest. At the same moment, Frank put a warning hand on his brother's arm. The gun went back into its holster and nothing more was said.

Hachita was smaller than McNeal, but it was a place where the telegraph ran through. The telegraph office was going to be the first stop for Lancer when he arrived. He was still enjoying Rabbi Vinburg's company. Lancer spent most of the morning laughing at the rabbi's mannerisms and tales. The rabbi definitely wasn't Orthodox, and he had a kindness about him that Lancer appreciated.

"Rabbi, where do you go from here? As I said, I'm going on to El Paso."

"I will stay right here in Hachita. It is a boom town and a mining town. Lots of silver and copper, and where there are such things, God must come. If God sees fit, I'll find a stream loaded with silver, and I will use that to build Him an altar."

"Or a temple?"

"You are a perceptive man, Lancer," the rabbi replied. "And by the way, I wasn't too asleep to get to the 'good parts.'"

The rabbi smiled as he drove his horse-drawn cart into the boom town. Lancer was grateful that he had met this man. But now he needed to find the telegraph office, so they said their goodbyes.

The telegraph office was not hard to find. The man in black tied up his horse and walked in. The clerk got up immediately and nodded in greeting to Lancer.

"I'd like to send a telegram to Tombstone, care of the local law --," Lancer began, but the clerk cut him off.

"Don't you want to know who is left, first?"

"I'm not sure, but you're probably right," Lancer said in a subdued tone. "What happened?"

"Before I tell you, whose side are you on?"

"Does it matter?"

"It might."

"Wyatt Earp is a friend of mine."

The clerk gave a sigh of relief. "Then you will be pleased to know he's alive and well. His brother Morgan was wounded but is okay. We heard Virgil took a flesh wound and Doc Holliday as well. But they are all fine."

"And?"

"And both Frank and Tom McLaury were killed and so was Billy Clanton. Ike Clanton and Billy Claiborne escaped injury. We got word the local police, one John Behan, I believe, tried to arrest the Earp brothers for murder."

Lancer was relieved but puzzled by Behan's response. He knew Behan wanted the Earps out of the way, but to charge them with murder was ridiculous. It would never stick.

"Good, good," Lancer told the clerk. "Send this message to Wyatt, please."

The clerk got his pencil and prepared to write.

"Heard the news," Lancer dictated. "Hope all is well. Watch your back. Will help if I can. Stay clear of JB."

The clerk nodded approvingly and Lancer paid him. Now Lancer was ready to resupply and head down to El Paso. He had his own gunfight awaiting him, or so he surmised. It was time to concentrate all his energy on the job ahead, whatever that job entailed. All he knew was that he was honor-bound to help Dallas Stoudenmire.

The two had fought nearly to the finish at the Battle of Franklin in Georgia, where the future marshal of El Paso was a young private under General Hood. Hood's forces battled Major General Schofield, under whom the man who would become known as Lancer was a young lieutenant. Hood's army was almost annihilated in the skirmish with Schofield's command, holding onto the city of Franklin after an early collapse.

When the fighting ended, six Confederate generals were dead and the Alabama 45th, of which Stoudenmire was a part, was nearly gone. The few remaining soldiers withdrew to Nashville after the Union victory at the Second Battle of Franklin in 1864. As fate would have it, Lancer and Stoudenmire met on the battlefield and shared a canteen. Stoudenmire had been wounded and was trying to reach safety. He'd crawled behind a berm near a stream.

Lancer's horse had been shot out from under him and he was dazed. His sword lay near the watering hole. As he crawled to get it, he heard the cock of a musket loading. He froze and found himself looking directly down the musket's barrel into the eyes of Dallas Stoudenmire. But the private was so weak, the rifle fell from his hands and he was about to collapse. The union officer realized the danger was probably over. He made an on-the-spot decision to help the Rebel youngster. Lancer took off his canteen, filled it at the watering hole and shared it with the wounded young man who was supposed to be his mortal enemy.

In an instant they became friends. They shared names and where they were from. After what seemed like forever, though it was really only a few minutes, they realized they needed to move back to their own lines. They would not see each other again until years later, when Stoudenmire was a member of the Texas Rangers.

By then Lancer was on an assignment from the 7th Cavalry and had made it down to the Texas panhandle on the orders of General Custer. Stoudenmire was in charge of supplying horses to the military. Together, he and Lancer corralled 125 wild horses for the Army. Remembering the canteen incident brought them together once again as friends, never to be forgotten. So when Stoudenmire in El Paso called upon Lancer in Tombstone, there was no question Lancer would go.

Lancer was a few miles outside El Paso when he passed the Manning Ranch. He had no inkling at that point just how the Mannings would fit into his reason for being there. But he was thirsty, and as chance would have it, he saw a man fixing a fence post -- a man who happened to be Jeff Manning.

"Excuse me, I'm heading for El Paso but I could sure use a drink of fresh water," Lancer called as he reined in Lincoln. "Might there be some close by?"

Manning looked up from the bottom of the fence. He wasn't a fan of strangers but he also wasn't someone who would deny another man a drink of water.

"Sure, just head down the road for about 200 yards and turn right, toward the main house. Ride up and ask for Rebo. Can't miss him. He's darker than any Mexican you'll find. Tell him Jeff sent you along. Fix you right up."

"Much obliged," Lancer said. "Then you must be Jeff."

Manning ignored him and kept on working. Lancer thought it rude but the man did agree to give him some water and that was all he needed for now.

Rebo was black as coal and Lancer picked him out right away. Seeing a rider coming, Rebo left the porch, where he was beating a rug, to come out and greet the stranger. Rebo, being a good judge of horses, was quick to admire Lincoln.

"Quite an animal you got there, mister. Yessiree, he's quite a handsome fella," Rebo called out even before Lancer greeted him.

"Thank you kindly. We've been together a long time," Lancer replied. "You must be Rebo."

"I is, but how you know my name?"

"Fella named Jeff told me to look you up. Need a little water, and Lincoln here is mighty dry too."

Rebo stood back and looked the horse up and down, his face lighting up.

"Lincoln, you say. I do declare you must have fought for the Union during the war. I mean, you got a proud horse with a proud name. You got to be a Union man."

Lancer smiled and nodded. Rebo took Lincoln by the reins and led the man and his horse to the water trough at the edge of the sprawling house. Lincoln knew a friendly face when he saw one and followed the man without hesitation. The giant black stallion began lapping up the water right away.

"Why don't you git down offa there and come on over," Rebo asked, looking up at Lancer. "Got some mighty fine lemonade on the porch. Just made. You like lemonade?"

"I do, especially on a hot day like today," Lancer said. "Thank you, Rebo."

The two men sat down on the porch and Lancer sipped the cool, lemon-flavored drink. Rebo poured him another.

"What business you got around these parts anyway? Horse business, I expect. You sure know that horse flesh," Rebo said. "By da way, they also call me Union. 'Cuz I took the last name o' Union when I freed up. Lots of folks took that last name, 'cuz Mr. Lincoln done freed us up."

Lancer sipped down the second glass and looked across the vast expanse known as Manning Ranch with a smile. He knew a lot of former slaves who took the name Union. It was common.

"Well, Rebo Union, I came to help an old friend who sent for me," he said.

"Well, it's always good to have a friend ta call on when you needs 'em, for sure," Rebo said with a smile. "Who ya friend?"

"Marshal Stoudenmire."

Rebo froze and dropped his glass. As it crashed to the floor, shards went everywhere and Lancer was startled. He jumped up and tried to help, but seeing the look in Rebo's eyes, he suddenly knew he'd stumbled upon something connected with the marshal's reason for calling on him. His pistol at the ready but still holstered, Lancer began glancing around for anyone else.

"I'm sorry, boss, but I thinks you better leave now," Rebo said, composing himself.

Just then Frank Manning came riding up from behind the house. He noticed the broken glass immediately, and seeing the stranger left him uneasy.

"What's going on here?" he said with a stern look. "Rebo?"

Rebo was uncharacteristically speechless so Manning turned to Lancer.

"What's this all about, and who are you?"

Lancer held out his hand to shake and Manning reluctantly reached over. He was confused about what was going on but was swiftly unconfused when Rebo blurted out the reason.

"He a friend of Marshal Stoudenmire, boss."

Manning quickly withdrew his hand and whipped out his gun. Lancer remained calm. There's always a reason a man pulls a gun over a few words, and this was neither the time nor place to find out.

"Who are you to Stoudenmire?"

Lancer stood his ground and thought quickly. He didn't want to give anything away, especially since he had no idea what he was in for, so he turned to history, his favorite subject.

"Old friends from the war, and it's a long story which I won't bore you with. We were on opposite sides but shared a watering hole in a friendly kind of way."

Manning lowered his gun but spoke to Lancer with a directness that left a lasting impression.

"Any friend of Dallas Stoudenmire is no friend of mine and is not welcome here. Now move on down the road. The next time I see you, I may have to kill you."

Lancer looked over at Rebo, who was still shaking. The man in black understood there was something here that did not add up. But he also knew that whatever it was would unfold later. As it turned out, it would not be long before Lancer found out the answer to this mystery.

El Paso is the only place in Texas with a mountain. Texas has several valleys but only one mountain. El Paso del Norte towers over the terrain below, highlighting the difference between New Mexico and Texas. There was talk of a railroad, but the rail barons seemed to consider El Paso like the rest of Texas -- the bastard child. So, there was no rail service, and the only way to get into and out of the area was by horse or wagon.

Since El Paso was so close to Mexico, it was off the beaten path. But that didn't matter to the folks who lived there and shared the Rio Grande as a border. The river shifted once in a great while, and the border moved with it, but it didn't seem to bother the cattle rustlers much. They were most active when the river was at its lowest point, in the winter months. Cattle could drown in the river if thieves tried to run them across in the spring or summer.

Lancer didn't think it was rustlers Stoudenmire was calling on him to help with. The marshal could get federal help to deal with Mexican bandits. It must be something bigger, and his reception at the Manning Ranch seemed to indicate a family feud. Once he got to town, the first stop would be the office of Dallas Stoudenmire.

Lancer and Lincoln arrived from the west. The river flowed steadily to their right. It was majestic even in the autumn. He'd only been to the great river once before, and it reminded him of other great rivers, just not as wide. Nothing seemed wider than the Mississippi, even the Thames in London or the Seine in Paris. The Yellow and the Yangtze were great rivers he'd seen as well. But with fewer people on its banks, the Rio Grande was much cleaner than all the others.

Lancer loved the water. He thought often of the excursions he'd taken across the ocean with his father. From the Atlantic to the Mediterranean, they were soothing travels. Of course, there were the occasional storms. But they were rare, at least on his youthful trips.

The lights of El Paso lay ahead, and it was dusk when he rode up to the marshal's office. The city was more than a frontier outpost, but the jail was still a jail. A light could be seen inside, and the gunman knew his old friend was still inside. His gut told him Stoudenmire had spent many a night at the jailhouse since asking for Lancer's help.

Lancer opened the door cautiously and found both barrels of a shotgun aimed at him. He raised his hands only to see the man holding the shotgun burst into laughter. It was Dallas Stoudenmire.

"You old son of a bitch, you nearly got yourself picked clean," the marshal razzed him.

"Probably not, you old Rebel," Lancer replied good-naturedly. "If I remember right, you couldn't hit the broad side of a barn if you were in it."

The two laughed and moved to the center of the room to greet each other with a bear hug.

"You are a sight for sore eyes," Stoudenmire said, holding his friend at arm's length. "Now I can finally get some sleep. Have any trouble along the way?"

As Stoudenmire went to the coffee pot and poured two cups, Lancer took off his coat and hat and pulled up the chair next to Stoudenmire's desk.

"None, really, until right before I got here. Seems I asked for water at the wrong ranch. Just outside of town."

"The Manning place!"

"I guess they're the reason I'm here, huh?"

Marshal Stoudenmire put his hand to his chin and rubbed his whiskers. "Yup."

Lancer began sipping the black coffee Stoudenmire handed him and waited for more of an answer. It took Stoudenmire a bit before finally coming through.

"Got James Manning in a cell back there," he said, pointing to the rear of the jailhouse. "Killed a man. Oh, it *may* have been in self-defense. But it wasn't *how* the man was killed. It was *who* got killed."

Lancer sat perplexed for a moment as Stoudenmire opened a bottle of whiskey. The marshal poured a bit of the stuff into Lancer's cup.

"A man's dead," Lancer said. "What does it matter who, if the shooting was legal?"

Stoudenmire wandered around the room, not wanting to answer but knowing he had to.

"The man was my brother-in-law, Doc Cummings," he blurted out. "The Manning clan and I haven't been on the friendliest of terms. Doc and James Manning got into it on the street. Doc was drunk, dead drunk, and he couldn't pull a pistol on his best day and he'd never ever hit anything. So when Manning got pushed, he waited until Doc put his hand even close to his gun and fired point-blank."

Lancer realized his friend was telling a tale that might be one-sided, but Stoudenmire was a lawman too. And Lancer knew that lawmen were considered expert witnesses and given extra leeway when it came to discretion. Lancer could see how the townspeople would view the killing of the family member of the marshal. They could also see how a pair of brothers who had bad blood with the marshal would want revenge. This was a difficult situation.

"Any witnesses? I mean, people who actually saw the killing?" Lancer asked.

Stoudenmire told him about Parsons and how the town felt about the marshal and how they felt about the Mannings. Parsons was a stooge caught in the middle. As far as Stoudenmire was concerned, Parsons was only siding with the Mannings because few people stood for the marshal. Parsons was a man with no family and no real job, and he and spent most of his time in the saloon begging for drinks. He was not credible, at least as far as Stoudenmire was concerned.

"Circuit judge will be here in two days and I'm just holding on until he gets here for trial," Stoudenmire said. "No way will a jury convict Jim Manning, so I've had the prosecutor ask for a trial by judge."

"Is that legal?"

"If I say it's legal, the town charter says I have the authority."

"From what I saw of the Mannings, I'd hate to be that judge. I think the first order of business for me is to make sure he gets here in one piece. Coming by stage?"

"Day after tomorrow."

"I presume the Mannings know that too?"

"Yep," Stoudenmire answered. "You want to go out and meet the stage?"

Lancer thought about it for a moment and decided it was probably a good idea. An attacker would find it easy to pick off the man riding shotgun, stop the stage and kill the judge or kidnap him. A man posted inside, a man who was good with a gun, might be just enough to ward off an attack. Lancer's mind was racing.

"Where and when would the Mannings try to ambush the stage, if indeed they were going to be so bold?"

"About 10 miles east of town there's a pass where the stage must go slow, or at least slow down enough to make it really dangerous," Stoudenmire said. "It's perfect for an ambush, and there is no way around it except to go 15 miles to the north or cross into Mexico, and no driver will even think about trying that."

The two men decided Lancer would ride beyond the pass, stop the stage, show a letter from the marshal and board it. A stable boy, Hart Williams, would ride along to bring back Lincoln. No need to have the great horse tied to the stage while they were trying to fend off attackers.

Stoudenmire nodded in approval. "Good, good. Now, tell you what, you go over to the hotel and get a good night's sleep, and I'll bunk here one more night."

"You sure?"

"Positive."

"By the way, how is Isabella taking this?"

"She's all bent up inside. Doc was her only brother. She hasn't stopped crying. I hope you being here will help her get past this."

Lancer hugged his old friend again and headed for the hotel.

CHAPTER FIVE

The room at the El Paso Inn was comfortable. If Lancer needed something more than comfort after a weeklong ride from Tombstone, he didn't show it. A soft bed, clean sheets and a wash basin were comfort enough. He was looking forward to a good night's sleep and breakfast, but he was still wide awake.

He washed up and was getting ready to settle into bed when a quiet knock came at the door.

Must be the stable boy, Lancer thought to himself.

He expected Stoudenmire had already summoned the young man and sent him over to introduce himself. But when Lancer answered the door, he could not have been more surprised. A beautiful young Mexican woman stood before him. Her long black hair crested her shoulders and disappeared down her back. Her eyes, black as coal, popped as she gave a sly smile. What on earth was this Latin beauty doing at his door?

"Señor Lancer?" she asked in a sultry tone.

"Yes, señorita, but I am a loss as to who is asking."

"Maria Esborra, Mr. Lancer," she said in a hushed voice so that no one else could hear. "But they call me Essie. And I am here to help you. May I come in?"

Lancer stood by the side of the door and pushed it open wider, allowing the Mexican beauty to enter. Her dress was that of a dance hall girl, and he surmised she worked at a local saloon, Rosa's Cantina. Why was she here? And who sent her? Those were questions that ran through his mind as he tried to keep from being overwhelmed by her immense beauty.

"To what do I owe the pleasure, and it is a pleasure, Señorita --?"

"Essie, you may call me Essie."

"Okay, Essie, what can I do for you?"

"It is not what you can do for me, but it is what I can do for you."

She moved closer to him. The smell of cheap perfume did nothing for him, but her hands were soft, and as they caressed his chest through his shirt, he began to feel something inside him wanting to pull her closer. Another aroma came from her, overcoming the perfume. It was the desire of a woman wanting a man. He realized at this very moment, she was actually in a desiring mood and might be forgetting her own mission.

As their lips met she melted in his arms. He took her with all his strength into his arms and the two meshed as they pressed each other's lips. In the back of his mind, Lancer was keeping close to his own instincts. What if she were really good at this and was just lulling him to sleep until she could pull a knife or a gun? He hoped he was wrong, but he'd been down that road before.

She continued to press his chest against her ample breasts and he could feel the welling up inside of him as her heart pounded faster. When she reached for his belt, he lifted her off the ground. She straddled his waist as they moved to the bed, where a night of pleasure unfolded.

It wasn't like Lancer to fall so quickly into romance, but then again it wasn't often such a beauty advanced from his door to his bed on her own, and in record time. If she was sent, and he believed she was, whoever sent her wanted information, especially on who Lancer was and why he was there. As they lay side-by-side in the afterglow of love -- she asleep, he awake -- he thought about who might be waiting for a report on him.

Lancer figured the Mannings had sent her, although it might be Stoudenmire. But why the latter when the former had all the reason in the world. Or could it be, maybe, just perhaps this goddess of a woman saw something she liked and wanted to taste the forbidden fruit? Lancer, a humble man when it came to such matters, decided it must be something else.

He fell into fitful slumber, only to be awakened at dawn as the morning light was about to come pouring in the window. Seeing that first gray glimmer, Lancer knew that if there were a clue in the room as to who Essie really was, he had to search fast. Her clothes were well-made, and as he squeezed the outer garment that lay on the nearby chair, he found nothing bulky or out of the ordinary. No knife, no gun. Not even a letter or piece of notepaper.

The small click of a gun hammer behind him stopped him cold.

"Looking for this, señor?" Essie asked. He turned to find her still in bed, pointing a derringer at him.

"Something like that, you might say."

"Well here it is, Mr. Lancer," she said, sliding off the bed and standing a few feet from the man she'd made love to hours earlier. "Turn around."

As he turned his back to her, he quickly surveyed the room. What advantage did he have, or perhaps more importantly, what disadvantage did she have?

No obvious answer came to mind, so he chose to stall by talking.

"So, what's this all about, anyway?"

"Why did you come here, to El Paso?"

"Now that's my business, and it *is* business," he answered turning again to face her. "Let me ask you, who sent you and why?"

She pulled back on the second barrel of the double-barreled gun. The click seemed louder this time.

"I'm asking the questions, and you don't have much choice in the matter," she said coldly. "Now I ask you again, who sent for you and what are you doing here?"

"No, those are two new questions, Señorita Essie," he said, trying to occupy her thoughts and distract her. "First you asked 'why did I come here' and now 'who sent me and why,' which while they may sound similar, they are not," he said, hoping to confuse the woman into letting her guard down. "So which is it, one, two or three, or perhaps all?"

She wasn't smiling, and as Lancer moved closer, she raised the small gun higher, but she also stepped back. Lancer knew he had her now. With lightning speed, his left foot lunged forward as his left hand grabbed her right hand that held the gun. He pushed the gun to his left as the weapon went off and in one swift motion grabbed her other arm with his free hand, putting both her arms in a vise grip.

"Now, Essie, are you going to tell me what it is *you* are doing here? Or are we going to cross the street and let Marshal Stoudenmire deal with you?"

"Let me go! You're hurting me!" she wailed.

"I will, when you give me some information," Lancer proclaimed as she struggled, "or so help me God, I'll march you right across the street right now as you are, in all your lovely nakedness!"

"You wouldn't dare!"

"Watch me!"

Lancer, wearing only his trousers, started pushing the naked woman toward the door. She fought to free herself but was powerless. Finally he picked her up and slung her over his shoulder. She kicked and screamed as they moved down the steps and across the lobby for all to see. The men watched and laughed while the women stood in horror.

"Young man, put that woman down!" yelled a woman in her elder years. "At least give her some decency!"

As he moved toward the door, he stopped and eyed the older woman up and down.

"Sorry, ma'am, she left her decency in my room last night before she pulled a gun on me," he answered.

The indignant woman stood for a moment, then giggled and stepped back. The cowboys in the lobby followed them out of the hotel and across the street. Men on horseback stopped in their tracks as Lancer marched through the dusty street with a naked woman over his shoulder. One woman walking with her small boy covered his eyes. A few men whistled. Finally, Lancer entered the marshal's office and closed the door behind him.

"What the hell! Lancer, what have you done?" Marshal Stoudenmire exclaimed in shock.

"You tell me, Dallas. This woman comes up to my room, seduces me, then pulls a gun on me. Now who is she, and what's this all about?"

Trying to hold back a chuckle, Stoudenmire pointed to the back cell.

"She's James Manning's sweetheart," he said.

Lancer had not thought of Manning -- not this Manning, anyway. He'd thought of the others trying to get information, but he didn't realize it was a woman in love who was trying to protect her man -- even to the point of giving all of herself to the man she thought was brought in to make sure her lover would face the gallows.

Essie stood in the middle of the cold room, shivering and buck naked. She used an arm to cover her breasts and a hand to cover her lower region. Lancer looked around the room and saw Stoudenmire's long coat hanging on the wall. He pulled it down and handed it to Essie, who forced a smile. She appreciated the gesture, although only for a moment.

"You can go see him now," Stoudenmire told her.

As she began to move, Lancer stopped her to search the coat. Inside a pocket he found a knife.

"Always remembered you carried a knife in your coat pocket, Dallas," he pointed out. Turning to Essie, he dismissed her. "Now go on." Essie stomped off to the jail cell to see her lover.

Lancer and Stoudenmire grinned at each other. Lancer shrugged. "Can't ever be too careful, now, can we?"

Stoudenmire poured a cup of coffee and Lancer indicated that he'd like one too. "However, I might want to get back to my room and get a little better dressed," he said, standing shirtless and barefoot in the middle of the office. He felt naked without his gun.

As the two men sipped coffee in the outer office, Essie kissed James through the bars of the jail cell. He'd fallen hard for the woman, and it was a sore point with his brothers. Yes, she was a dance hall girl and therefore had slept with many men, but he loved her and she loved him. Her past was going to stay in the past, if the brothers would let it. It was the only bone of contention among them.

"Essie, why did you come here?" he asked after the first kiss.

"They brought me here -- he brought me here," she burst out.

"Who? Who is 'they' and who is 'he'?"

"That Señor Lancer," she said. "He's the marshal's hired gunman. I fear he's going to kill you."

He held her through the bars and tried to calm her fears.

"No, Essie. I heard Lancer was coming, and I don't fear him. He's a good man, a man who respects the law, and if anything, he's here to make sure I get a fair trial. Don't worry. With him here, I'm sure Marshal Stoudenmire will be forced to let me go. Besides, Doc pulled first."

Manning looked away as he said the final line, and that wasn't lost on Essie.

"You are not sure."

"I *am* sure, but he was drunk and I was angry," he said, bowing his head. "I guess I might have avoided a fight, maybe used my fists and taken his gun. It would have been easy, but -- well, it was a bad night. I was angry and things got out of hand. I know he was no match for me or any man who knew even a little about how to use a gun. I *am* sorry it happened. But... I *won't* hang for it!"

She held him again through the bars. She loved James Manning and knew of his battle with his brothers. Here she was -- a dance hall girl, and even worse, a Mexican. They were white and had come from Missouri with their father when they were children. He was a border stater and was as conflicted about slavery as anyone living on the border.

Still, the Manning patriarch would not have approved of her, and it had trickled down to at least two of his sons. But James was different. He was humble and loving, and while he had the famous Manning temper, he was not as calculating as Frank nor as impulsive as Jeff. Jeff followed wherever Frank went. James, on the other hand, had a mind of his own. He wanted to divide the ranch among the brothers and work his own land in a cooperative way with the other two. Frank would not allow it. It was James who had insisted on hiring Rebo. Rebo would go with him and Essie when the time came.

Essie hugged her man one more time and a passionate kiss followed before she left. She was happy he did not ask her to take off the coat. In fact, he was so happy to see her that he didn't even notice what she was wearing. It was a good thing, she thought, because if James knew what she'd done with Lancer the night before....

Lancer sat at breakfast in the El Paso Inn's coffee room. A meal of biscuits and gravy along with a side of tortillas and salsa graced his plate. He'd never had the combination before, but the savory with the hot was tasty. It reminded him of the northwest corner of China. When he was a young man, he'd traveled the Silk Road for month with his father. The area was rich in peppers and other spices not seen in Peking or other Chinese cities to the east.

He remembered the time he was introduced to a young Chinese girl about his age. The well-built teenager was just beginning to explore the first fruits of pleasure in his life, and the time spent with Chu Chow was as promising as it could be. While the relationship blossomed over the course of four days, fortunately for the two of them, it was never consummated.

Chow's father was a businessman. He was also a warlord, and along the Silk Road, warlords ruled over the businessmen. Bringing a caravan filled with goods from Europe to China was a nasty piece of business, and Chow's father was not above getting his share of the proceeds. He cut lucrative deals with companies in the Western Hemisphere, including Lancer's father.

If the two teens had been caught together, one of two things would have happened -- marriage or death. Either way, his father's business would be gone, and the young man feared that outcome. Even at a young age, he had a sense of responsibility. Knowing the bad outcomes outnumbered the potential joy of the moment, he had to put his feelings aside and let the young lady down without fulfilling the desires of two exploring youths. She understood that as much as he did, so while the feeling and the understanding were mutual, so was the teenage disappointment they felt. He never forgot her, and he hoped that feeling was shared.

The loud, needling voice of Frank Manning interrupted his reverie. "Excuse me, Mr. Lancer, I think I told you your kind wasn't welcome around here. Now, I don't know what business you have here, but if your business extends to Marshal Stoudenmire, then I suggest you leave. No, I'm *ordering* you to leave."

Lancer continued eating, not even looking up to acknowledge Frank Manning. This only riled the man even more.

"I said leave, and leave now!"

Lancer reached for his coffee cup and took a sip. Manning slapped it away and the cup went flying, crashing on the floor in a liquid mess. Everyone in the place stopped what they were doing. Several people got up and stepped outside, fearing a fight with bullets was about to break out. Lancer sat calmly in his chair.

"Now, I wish you hadn't done that, mister," he said. "I was actually enjoying that cup of coffee.

You see, they put a little chicory in the coffee here, and I happen to like chicory in my coffee."

"Well, they make a specialty of it down in New Orleans, so if you get on your horse and ride right now, you might be there in time for supper tomorrow," Manning sneered. His right hand was now closer to his handgun than a moment ago.

Lancer saw it but knew he had the upper hand.

"But you see, I paid for *that* cup of coffee and the owner of this establishment expected to see me finish it," Lancer said calmly as he shifted slightly in his chair. Suddenly and with lightning speed, his left fist struck a hard blow into Manning's groin and the man doubled up, trying in vain to go for his weapon. As Manning curled, Lancer reached for Manning's gun, freed it from its holster and used his other hand to give a hard single chop to the back of Manning's neck. Manning fell to the ground in a heap, still holding his private parts.

Lancer bent down, grabbed Manning by the nape of the neck and whispered loudly in his ear.

"Now, Mr. Manning, like I said, I'm going to finish my coffee and my breakfast without being disturbed. And you, my good man, are going to walk out of here, or crawl if you must, and go back to your ranch, and leave me the hell alone."

Manning could not move. Lancer got up and deposited Manning's handgun on the counter in front of the clerk.

"Don't give this back to him until he leaves and comes back to town on another day. By then maybe he'll have cooled off enough to handle it. Oh say, can I get another cup of coffee?"

"On the house, Mr. Lancer," came the reply. "And my chicory is better than the stuff in Louisiana by far. Thank you kindly."

Lancer raised the coffee cup as if in a silent toast, took a sip and smiled broadly. The clerk was right.

CHAPTER SIX

Marshal Stoudenmire and Lancer worked out the details of where to meet the stage and the traveling judge. The stage would hit the proper spot about three o'clock in the afternoon, so Lancer spent the rest of the morning preparing for his ride, checking his rig and getting a shotgun and a long rifle from the marshal. If the stage were attacked, he could do some real damage from a distance with those guns and ward off the attackers.

The livery stable was at the end of town, and young Hart Williams was already standing by, ready with Lincoln and another horse. Lancer looked at the boy, merely 17, and while the lad stood long and rangy, Lancer hoped he was also smart as a whip. He didn't want anything left to chance. All he wanted was for the Williams boy to ride with him, drop him off and bring Lincoln back to the livery.

"You Hart Williams?" Lancer asked in greeting.

"I am, sir. You must be the famous Lancer."

"Well, I *am* Lancer. It's up to history to judge if there is another part to that description," he chuckled. "Marshal tell you what you are to do?"

"Yes sir, he did. Ride with you and bring your horse back here. Seems simple enough."

"Good. Then let's ride, son."

The pair rode off at a slight gallop, heading down the eastern road out of town. It would take them an hour to get to the rendezvous spot. Another reason for Hart coming along was that the driver and the shotgun man had no clue they were coming. But they knew Hart because the driver was Hart's father. Lancer loved it when a plan came together like that.

As they were leaving town, Lancer noticed the rifle strapped to Hart's horse. And Hart noticed Lancer looking at it.

"Single shot musket," Hart said. "It belonged to my dad's father. Never leaves my side on a ride."

Lancer felt uncomfortable about that, since he didn't know whether the boy was good with a weapon or merely had a strong sense of false security. But there was little he could do. The boy was nearly a man, and such decisions were to be made by his father first. The ride out of town was an easy one, and Lancer hoped it would be an uneventful one as well. He'd just as soon not need to use any guns. Getting the judge to town in one piece was the goal. It wouldn't do if the judge arrived and couldn't perform his duties.

Lancer expected plenty of trouble, though. He knew Frank Manning was not going to let his brother go to prison, or worse yet, hang. Lancer knew, too, while there was a chance a judge might find James guilty, there was better than an even chance he'd walk. What Lancer did not know was that Frank Manning was recruiting a small army to make sure his brother got off, and the army was filled with men with a price on their head.

"How on earth did you ever get the name of Hart, son?" Lancer queried the boy riding alongside him.

Hart lowered his head for a moment and then perked up with his head held high, like he'd just realized something.

"You see, Mr. Lancer, the man I refer to as my dad really isn't my father," Hart began. "I'm a town boy. Jessup Williams took me in. I didn't have a name. He found me lying in the stable when I was just a couple weeks old, the story goes. Whoever was my mother left me there and sent a note to the stage office. Mr. Williams, my dad, was the first to read it."

Lancer was touched. He'd known a few "town boys" in his time. Some went on to be good citizens raised by good people. Others went on to a life of crime. They'd been raised by strict, often mean, people who were the only option for such a child when no one else had room for another mouth to feed.

Lancer liked Hart and pursued his questioning.

"That's a right fine story, and you turned out okay, it looks like. But it doesn't answer my question about how you came about your name."

"Easy. My father was related to Henry Clay."

"I don't get the connection."

"Henry Clay was related to my father and my dad liked him a lot, but Mr. Clay didn't want anyone named after him, for some odd reason which I don't understand. I mean, if someone wants to honor you by naming their son after you, you should like that, right?"

Lancer nodded.

"So, I don't get it, but Clay's wife was related to a woman named Elizabeth Preston McDowell, whom my dad also knew and liked. And thank the good Lord above he didn't name me Elizabeth," Hart said with a smile.

Lancer could hardly hold back a laugh and was impressed by the boy's sense of humor.

"Go on."

"Well, Elizabeth was married to a famous U.S. senator named Thomas Hart Benton, and my mom hated the name of Thomas. Seems she once had a beau by that name. And Benton was not to my father's liking. So Hart it is, and there you have it."

Lancer felt very entertained by Hart's explanation and suspected this young man had a bright future. Greatness sometimes begins with a name.

Then Hart asked the one question Lancer rarely answered. "And how did you come by Lancer?"

"It's a long story and we have a short ride to the rendezvous point," Lancer said, speeding Lincoln's gallop a bit.

Hart understood he'd asked the wrong question.

When they reached the top of the hill, the spot Stoudenmire said was good for an ambush, they saw the stage down in the gully wash, far in the distance. They took to a gallop right away, knowing they needed to stop the stage before it got to this point.

"Look, riders ahead and coming fast!" Jessup Williams called out to his partner on the stage, pointing ahead.

"Bandits?" Asked the messenger guard.

Williams was taking no chance. "Let's pick up the pace, and you get that scatter gun ready."

The two horsemen rode like the wind, hoping to get to the stage before it had to slow down. Hart took off his hat and waved it high over his head, trying to let his father know it was him. It worked.

"Hey, that's Hart out there," the messenger guard yelled. "What's he doing?"

The driver recognized his son, and seeing the smile on his face was good enough reason for him to slow down and pull to a stop. As they did, the two riders pulled alongside.

"Dad, this is Lancer. The marshal sent him out to escort the judge to town."

Jessup Williams reacted with surprise. "Escort the judge? You expectin' trouble?"

The elder Williams was a beefy man who had seen a rough life. He'd been held up several times on his runs and even carried a bullet in his shoulder.

But he'd always gotten the stagecoach through. He did not relish what might lie ahead.

"Mr. Lancer, I'm Hart's father, Jessup Williams. I hope you weren't counting on him to go along with us "

"No, he has strict orders to ride ahead and take my horse with him," Lancer assured him. "We'll stay here for a bit to let him get a head start. I want to make sure he passes that hill before they get wise someone might be riding along inside."

Hart snapped his fingers with an idea.

"Dad, you remember that old Indian trail? It sort of parallels the main road?"

Jessup knew where Hart was going and nodded.

"I'll take that. I should be past the hill in about 20 minutes. That won't leave you with any worries about me."

"Good idea, son."

Lancer liked Hart more and more. He motioned to the boy to get started and he climbed into the coach and faced the passenger. Judge Cole Blakemore had been listening to the talk.

"What's going on, young fella?" Blakemore asked. "You going to ride along to protect me from outlaws? I know they hang out around here."

"Not so much outlaws, Your Honor. More like a family feud," Lancer said politely. "You are going to try a man for murder, and his brothers don't like it one bit. Get my meaning?"

The judge leaned back and sighed. He knew he was in for a murder trial but he had not seen this coming.

Lancer leaned out the door and yelled, "Let's go!" to Jessup Williams. The whip crack underscored the seriousness of the job ahead. The horses pulled their weight in quick fashion, but even the animals seemed to sense what was ahead. The steep hill was a place they were going to slow down. They'd done it dozens of times before, and as horses went, these were as smart as any.

Lancer kept a close eye on the terrain, looking for anything out of the ordinary. His time spent with Custer had served him well. A scout for the most part, a reconnaissance specialist, he could spot a clump of trees that seemed to be hiding danger or bushes that didn't quite look right.

"If you see riders near the top of the hill, slow down only as you need to," Lancer yelled to the driver. "I'll fire some rounds. That should get you to a spot where you can pick up speed again. Make sure you keep low."

Williams knew exactly what Lancer meant. The gunmen would not expect a shot from inside the coach. It should be just enough to give the driver the edge to plow through. Williams thought Lancer's plan was brilliant -- if it worked. If not, none of them would be home for supper that night.

Sitting in a clump of trees at the top of the hill were six riders. They wore masks, as bandits often do, but they were not there to rob the stage. At least that was not their primary goal. Frank Manning had instructed the hired guns to take no prisoners. They were to kill everyone and take the strongbox to make it look like a robbery. Manning had learned from a friend at the stage line that the judge was the only passenger.

Lancer crouched down inside the stage and told the judge to get on the floor. Peering cautiously out a corner of the window, he spied movement in the trees at the top of the hill and shouted up to the driver.

"To the right, the trees! Get ready to ride!"

Williams nonchalantly looked to his right, trying not to be obvious. He saw the same thing Lancer saw. The riders broke for the stage, guns drawn. As the stage started to slow, the lead gunslinger fired at the messenger, killing him instantly. Without missing a beat, Lancer fired and dropped the lead gunman dead to the ground.

That was the cue for Williams to hit the reins and hit them hard. The rest of the attackers were startled, and in their confusion, Lancer dropped two more. The remaining three retreated for cover at full gallop as the stage raced onward. Lancer knew the gunslingers would likely come after the stage once they regrouped. He was correct. Now he had to shoot with a rifle from a moving stage.

One gunman rode directly behind the stage, cutting off Lancer's view. Lancer wasn't able to get a clean shot, while at the same time rapid gunfire was coming uncomfortably close. Despite the shots missing their mark, they forced Lancer to keep his head down. He was too far away to use the shotgun, and the rifle was unsteady. The three gunmen bore down on the rear of the stage.

Suddenly a loud noise came from the back of the coach. One of the gunmen had leaped from his horse and was clinging to the cargo hold. Now the shotgun would come in handy. Lancer grabbed it and fired one shot point-blank into the rear of the stage. It broke through the paneling and the cowboy flew off the coach to his doom.

The other two were not deterred. A shot nearly killed the judge, tearing his hat off his head and grazing his scalp.

"Blood, blood, I'm shot!" Blakemore yelled out.

"A flesh wound!" Lancer yelled back.

Judge Blakemore, somewhat relieved, laid even lower in the stage. The horsemen were close.

A shot rang out but this time it wasn't from a handgun, it was a rifle -- a musket. Lancer peered out the window just in time to see one of the gunslingers fall. The lone remaining gunman turned and took off in the opposite direction. Not long afterward, the stagecoach came to a stop. Hart Williams came running up to the side and looked in.

"Everybody okay in there?" he asked anxiously.

"Everybody is, indeed." Lancer replied. "Nice shooting, kid."

Hart Williams grinned to say how much he appreciated getting Lancer's approval. He mounted his horse and took the lead in escorting the stage and his father, along with the precious cargo, the few miles to El Paso.

Lancer stayed inside with Judge Blakemore.

"Mighty fine shooting, mister," Blakemore said. "You got a name?"

"Lancer."

"*The* Lancer, out of Tombstone?"

"The same."

"Nasty business up there in Tombstone," Blakemore said. "You heard? The local sheriff, or marshal, or whatever he is, arrested the Earps and charged them with murder. Doc Holliday too. Damn fools. Earp's been running roughshod over people for years and no one ever paid it no mind as long as they kept the bad guys outta Dodge."

"Wyatt and the boys are pretty smart. You think it will stick?"

"Not a chance. Not if it's done legal. Besides, they should have enough friends to make a difference, if they get a jury that's not hand-picked by friends of the McLaurys. You know the family?"

"I do, and they've always treated me fairly," Lancer replied.

"But you make your living with a gun, so it stands to reason," Blakemore pointed out.

"Guns are only used when necessity makes their use the only option. 'Let gentleness my strong enforcement be; In the which hope I blush and hide my sword.' "

The judge knew immediately which play Lancer was quoting from. "Ahh, *As You Like It* by Shakespeare. You are a man of letters, are you not, Mr. Lancer?"

Lancer smiled as he began cleaning his pistol for the arrival in El Paso. The judge noticed the crossed lances on the holster and thought for a moment before asking another question.

"The meaning of the design of your holster, Lancer," he began. "May I inquire of its origin?"

Lancer had already evaded a question from Hart about his past. But he figured if the judge wanted to know, it might be best to oblige.

"I was always thrilled with the Bengal Lancers in India, their pomp, their circumstance and the bravery they showed in the conquest, if you can call it that, of India," he said. "There was something about them that stood out. Class, gallantry and a boldness that made them unique. I vowed, as a young boy visiting India, I would find my way to a similar lofty state of mind as a grownup."

"Thus the name 'Lancer,' I gather?"

Lancer looked out the window before answering.

"Partially. But it is where the holster design comes from, and I believe that's the question you asked."

The judge knew when to back off. "You are correct, and nothing more need be said. Some other time, perhaps."

Lancer smiled, for he had given, but not too much. He was a complicated man with a complicated past, and while he didn't need to be doing what he did for a living, he did it well. Doing things well was what Lancer strived for, and so far this mission was going well.

A crowd gathered as the stage pulled into El Paso. A man who'd been aboard the stage was dead, and he was a man they did not know. The new shotgun messenger was Robert Rheems of San Antonio. He was new to the stage company and it was only his second run. He'd left behind a wife and a small child, with another on the way. Now he was deceased, but so was the man who had taken his life.

The mayor of El Paso, the Honorable Rico Estrada, immediately put in motion an effort to raise money for the Rheems family. Lancer let it be known he would contribute $1,000 but he insisted that Estrada list it as anonymous. His generosity was great, but his humble spirit was greater. The mayor obliged, and soon he announced the town had raised more than $2,000 to give to the widow. It would help.

As the town buzzed about the stagecoach attack, Frank Manning stood watching from the window of the saloon. He was angry and it showed. His brother Jeff came up to him and spoke just a bit too loudly about the fact that the judge had arrived alive.

"Hush," Frank ordered his younger brother. "You want to tip them off? Shut up and go about your business. I'll handle this."

"Handle it?"

"I said I'll handle it," Frank shot back. "The first plan failed but the second one won't."

"Meanwhile, James rots in a jail cell," Jeff replied heatedly. "And the trial is coming up. What are you planning to do now?"

"I'm thinking."

Minutes later, Jeff and Frank Manning were seen riding out of town at a gallop. It was obvious to

Lancer they were behind the stagecoach attack, and Marshal Stoudenmire had the same thought.

"Mighty nice thing the mayor did today, getting the money raised so fast," Stoudenmire said from behind his desk to his friend. "Of course, you wouldn't know anything about that, now would you?"

Lancer remained quiet.

"I hear Frank Manning is rounding up a bunch of hired guns to take his brother out of here," Stoudenmire continued. "Think he'll wait until after the trial?"

"Don't know why he should. He's convinced you're going to hang James, no matter what."

"I might," said the marshal. "After all, he did kill a man, and even if you call it manslaughter and not murder, we're talking prison. Think he should get that?"

Lancer turned to his old friend with a bit of irritation.

"That's your emotions talking, Dallas, not the marshal's office."

Stoudenmire got up to stand face-to-face with his friend. "Same thing in this case. Got to keep law and order in this town, and the Mannings are doing everything they can to stop that from happening. Now, you saw what happened. You think they'll stop at killing a man? Why, they'd kill half this town if it meant something to them, and half the townspeople are their friends. So, yes, I'm emotional, but I'm also practical. Get the Mannings out and El Paso is a nice, peaceful town. Hell, I'd even retire here."

Lancer was half convinced, but he also knew there was a good chance James Manning was innocent of the charges of both murder and manslaughter. He'd wait for the judge to decide. The trial was going to start soon, and if it went badly, there would be a town to defend.

"Maybe I'll start with a little reconnaissance," Lancer began. "Go out there and see what's happening."

"You want me to go with you?"

"No you stay here. They may try to break him out."

Lancer had run into well-organized gangs of gunmen before, and he wasn't afraid of what might happen. Still, he needed to be cautious. He knew Frank Manning was a man who laid out a plan and thought things through. Maybe Manning wouldn't want to mess with Lancer, for fear of defeat. Lancer had a reputation, and a man with a good reputation had friends, lots of them. Why stir up trouble and pick a fight? Besides, Manning had already done exactly that and had gotten his butt whipped. Lancer didn't think he'd go for a second round very quickly.

The ride out to the Manning Ranch was not difficult. No one would contest Lancer's right to ride the main road. When he got to the gate of the huge spread, Lincoln began to behave a bit differently. The great horse seemed to sense something amiss, and Lancer knew to trust his steed's judgment. Lancer, too, felt something in the air. His best guess was that he was being watched, by someone close-by.

A man with a rifle drawn was coming up from behind, as quietly as possible. He was a native American, walking softly. Lancer had missed him but Lincoln had not. The great horse kicked back with a force that knocked the man to the ground and sent his rifle flying through the air.

"He doesn't like someone sneaking up behind him, and neither do I," Lancer declared, his gun drawn and aimed directly at the man. "Now get out here in front where I can see you."

The man obeyed and slowly walked forward to the house where the Mannings lived. Three men armed with rifles came from the side of the house. Lancer's handgun was still drawn. The men cocked their rifles but Lancer didn't budge.

"Put your rifles away. You'll all be dead before you get off a shot," came the voice of Frank Manning from the doorway. "Do it! Do it now!"

The men put their rifles down and Lancer holstered his pistol.

"Much obliged, Manning," Lancer said, swinging off of his horse.

"Not to worry. I don't like blood all over my front porch," came the cool reply. "No matter whose blood it is. Now, what's your business here?"

"To talk."

"I'm listening."

At that point a man moved from around the side of the house. Lancer recognized him as the lone surviving gunman who had attacked the stage.

"Manning, you've lost five men today and are about to lose a sixth," Lancer said sternly. "The judge is safe. Your brother will get a fair trial, and all I want you to do is let the trial happen."

"And you think my brother will get a fair trial for killing the marshal's kin?" Manning asked in disbelief. "You, mister, are naive."

The stagecoach attacker tried to appear nonchalant as his hand inched toward his holstered gun. Lancer saw him out of the corner of his eye and decided he wasn't going to give up any advantage.

"I'm not naive about that, Manning. But I do know Marshal Stoudenmire. He understands the situation, and he wants the judge to make sure justice is done fair-and-square. But you have to let the law take its course."

Manning noticed what Lancer noticed about the gunman and slowly moved up behind him. As the man reached for his gun, Manning grabbed his arm and forced the weapon back into his holster, even as Lancer's weapon cleared leather without being fired. Manning decked the gunman with one punch and held his gun in his hand.

"You see, Lancer, we take care of our own down here. And I'm going to make sure my brother doesn't hang for a killing that was self-defense. Now, I've said enough, so move on down the road. We'll be meeting again real soon."

Lancer holstered his gun and slowly turned his attention to the other men. He counted six, but knew it was probably at least twice that many and growing. He mounted Lincoln and rode off quietly. Manning gave the man back his gun and called the others into the house for a meeting.

Once outside the gate and out of sight from the Manning home, Lancer saw Rebo approaching.

"Mr. Lancer, you got a minute for me?" the black man pleaded.

Lancer nodded and Rebo came up alongside him.

"Mr. Lancer, I gots to tell ya, I heard Mr. Frank talking last night," Rebo began. "Seems they got lots o' folks coming in from all over."

"How many, Rebo?"

"I'd say 20 at least, maybe mo', maybe 30. I can't rightly say for sure, but I heared Mr. Jeff and Mr. Frank arguing about having enough men to do the job to get Mr. James outta the jail after the trial."

Lancer had guessed what was going to happen, and Rebo's information confirmed it. He'd ride back into town and discuss it with Marshal Stoudenmire.

CHAPTER SEVEN

"That's a lot of firepower!" Marshal Stoudenmire exclaimed as Lancer told of his meeting at the Manning Ranch and the conversation with Rebo. "I may have to call in the federal boys. But they'd never get here in time."

Lancer poured himself another cup of coffee and reached into the marshal's desk for the whiskey bottle. He added a strong shot to his cup as he sat down in the marshal's chair. These two presumptuous actions didn't disturb Stoudenmire. He knew Lancer was trying to figure out how to defend the town and to make sure they all lived through the day.

Stoudenmire realized, too, that Lancer knew military tactics. This was a key reason he'd sent for Lancer. The lawman understood he might have to face a small army before it was all over, and his own military skills didn't match Lancer's.

Lancer sipped his coffee slowly. "How many men can you count on to deputize and make a real stand?"

"Not many. The Mannings have their friends all over this town. Even if we could build a good unit, Frank Manning would know exactly our strength."

"How many?" Lancer insisted.

Stoudenmire held out his hand to count on his fingers quickly ticking off two.

"I got two guards at the judge's place of business. They are full-time deputies. Hand-picked. I would say maybe 10 men added to that."

"That gives us a small army of 14 guns," Lancer said. "It may not sound like a match, but I think we'd have the element of surprise, and definitely the upper hand when it comes to positioning."

Stoudenmire could see Lancer's mind going to work to get everyone through the coming fight with as little injury as possible.

"The high ground?" the lawman asked.

Lancer nodded.

"There are five two-story buildings in the center of town, right around here," Lancer said, pointing his hand in a circular motion above his head. "Long rifles, second-story windows and roof tops, three men inside. We'd have a good chance at defending the prisoner and ourselves."

Lancer looked around at the jailhouse itself. It was sturdy, and there were slots to serve as gun ports when the shutters were closed. It would take a small army with a howitzer to break through the front. The rear could be covered by a single gunman. Dynamite or nitro was a fear, but Frank and Jeff Manning probably wouldn't risk injuring their brother by doing that. They would have to assume the marshal would put James in a place where he could easily get killed if the brothers went too far.

"Okay, recruit whatever men you can and we'll make a stand if the Mannings try anything," Lancer said. "There is always a chance James will get off, but I want to be prepared for the worst should the judge convict him. "

At the Manning Ranch, the numbers were growing as the day drew near for the trial. Frank Manning was paying top dollar, and he was recruiting the worst of the worst for this job. They came from all over Texas and Arizona. Bandits, bounty hunters, ex-military who couldn't find their way after the war. They were all part of Manning's Army.

Frank and Jeff sat down to dinner. As Rebo began to serve them, a knock came at the door. The man doing the knocking didn't wait for an invitation. He just walked right in.

"You try waiting for an answer when you knock?" Jeff said sarcastically.

"The only invitation I need carries six bullets and spins off the cartridges faster than anyone I've ever seen," Big Jay Riley said as he stood staring down Jeff. "Just try me." Frank knew better and quickly defused the situation between his brother and the killer he'd hired.

"No need to get testy, now, is there?" Frank said politely. "Sit down. Have a cup. Break bread with us. Rebo, get Mr. Riley a plate."

Riley wasn't moved by the sudden hospitality, but he wasn't turning down homemade biscuits and gravy along with a nice slab of steak. He relaxed and pulled up a chair as Rebo brought out another plate.

The conversation started slowly, but when it turned to the possible opposition in El Paso, Riley grew angry.

"I've always wanted to get Lancer in my sights," he said. "Just one time. That would do it."

Jeff sat quietly while Frank listened and poured a glass of brandy for his guest.

"Truth be told, I hope they convict your brother and we have to go in. I'll get my shot at Lancer for sure."

Riley took a swig of the brandy and turned up his nose. "Women and old men drink this stuff. You got any whiskey?"

Frank glanced over at Rebo, who immediately pulled a bottle from the shelf and poured it for Riley. The big man gulped it down as Frank watched.

"Yep, just one time and BANG!"

Riley began to belly laugh at the thought of killing Lancer. The Manning brothers looked at him with alarm. They wanted their brother freed. This man only wanted to kill the messenger. Frank quickly decided he was okay with that, as long as his brother was the first order of business. Whatever grudge Riley had with Lancer could take place after James was free.

Lancer was a bold but cautious man. It was the caution he felt he needed to rely on now. He was going to help recruit the necessary men who would be willing to stand and fight the Mannings. The odds were going to be long, but the element of surprise and a wall of cover would help even things up. He hoped it would be enough to make the stand for El Paso.

He decided to pay a visit to Rosa's Cantina -- and Essie. She might know something, even though she was not close to Frank or Jeff. Still, she knew James very well, and James understood where his brothers were coming from. There might be some insights to be had by talking to the Mexican beauty.

Rosa's Cantina was a place most of the regular range riders stayed away from. It catered to a more ethnic clientele. The cowboys who came into town on a cattle drive might stop by if they had a hankering for a black or Mexican woman. But most of the men preferred to spend their time at the bigger and fancier saloon down the street.

Rosa's was at the end of town and was distinguished by loud music with an obvious south-of-the-border flair. Mariachis played at night. A piano was part of the décor, but there never seemed to be a piano player in the house.

Lancer walked the length of Main Street to the cantina. He stopped outside, listening to the raucous music. A tall, well-dressed man also stood near the doorway, two guns heeled and acting like you didn't want to mess with him. Lancer soon felt a finger poking him in the chest.

"Going somewhere, señor?" the tall man asked.

His English was polished but his accent gave away his nationality as Mexican.

Lancer looked down at the finger holding sway on his black vest. He looked up to see the man nonchalantly putting a cigarette to his lips. Lancer fished out a match from above his gun belt. With precision and speed, the Mexican whipped his pistol out of his holster and put it to Lancer's gut.

"Need a light, señor?" Lancer asked calmly as he struck the match against the crossed lances on his holster.

The match flared brightly as the Mexican smiled cautiously and holstered his gun. He leaned into Lancer's match, inhaled and blew a puff of smoke into the street. He wanted to blow it right into Lancer's face, but the man from Tombstone had a reputation that preceded him. The tall stranger stepped out of the way, and Lancer stepped confidently into the cantina.

As he did so, the music suddenly trailed off. Silence cracked the noise of the barroom. Time seemed to stand still as Lancer surveyed the room. The bar was to his left, the band was in front of him, and to his right was the stairway to the brothel. About 15 tables crowded the main room, and each was filled. Some of the men looked well-dressed, others were ranchers who had come in for a drink and a game of cards.

Rosa's voice broke the silence. "I wondered when you would get around to us." She approached him from behind the bar. "Señor Lancer, I presume?"

Lancer nodded as Rosa took him by the arm and led him to a doorway next to the bar. Before entering the doorway, she waved her hand at the band and the music began anew. The room filled with chatter again, and Lancer followed Rosa into her office.

Lancer decided to break the ice by tossing a compliment her way. "You pull in a rather large audience."

Rosa was round, short and had seen more than her share of trouble, both with men and the law. She didn't like the law or how the Americans treated the Mexicans, but she obeyed it. She had no use for men who abused women, and she wouldn't allow that sort of behavior in her establishment. And there was no mistaking it, the cantina was *her* establishment. Lancer suspected he would grow to like this proprietress.

"Sit down, Señor Lancer," she offered.

He sat across the desk from her. She was dressed like a high-class madam, although her ladies covered a wide range of classiness and classlessness. It was part of the trade. Some men liked the girl next door, others liked the whore at the door. Rosa didn't care, as long as the men left their money and left the girls in the same shape as they found them.

It was said Rosa had killed three men who pulled a knife on one of her ladies of the night. They never got to the cutting. Rosa plugged two of them. A third man died later, minus his member. Rosa testified at her own trial that she would have shot the other two in the groin as well, but there was little time to take aim in a life-and-death situation. The jury, made up solely of white men, saw her point. Some of them were her customers.

"Whiskey or brandy?" she asked.

"Depends on the brand, ma'am."

"For you, only the finest brandy will do. As long as you are here for the reason I think you are here."

"And what might that be?"

Rosa went to the safe on her wall, took out a large key hidden in the folds of her dress and opened the safe to reveal several bottles of spirits. She pulled out a bottle of Napoleon Cognac 1812.

"Napoleon the First had a brother, Jerome," she said.

"His youngest brother, if memory serves me correctly," Lancer said. When Rosa nodded in agreement, he added, "Ah, so you knew that, didn't you?"

"Yes, but I am impressed you did as well." Rosa took the bottle out of the safe.

She motioned to Lancer to grab a couple of glasses off the shelf on the other wall and he obliged her. When he set them on her desk, she pulled the cork and began the pouring. The aroma drifted sweet and fine into his nostrils. As they each picked up a glass and raised them, Rosa offered a toast.

"To the victor go the spoils, Señor Lancer, and may the victor be the man who treats people the way they are meant to be treated." Rosa held her glass high.

"I'll drink to that, Señora Rosa." They clinked glasses and sipped the nearly 70-year-old delicacy.

"Just Rosa, please, and may I call you Lancer?"

He grinned and she knew she was on the right track with this man who wore a single gun and rode a shining black stallion.

"So, how can I help?" she asked in a business-like tone.

"I want to talk with Essie, to see what she knows about what's going on at the Manning Ranch. I know she's friendly with James Manning."

Rosa laughed as if she knew something. Lancer wasn't expecting this, and the look of surprise on his face did not go unnoticed by Rosa. "I'm laughing because she is also 'friendly' with you, Lancer."

The man in black arched his eyebrows in surprise.

She laughed again. "Oh go on, sir, don't you think these girls talk among themselves? When they get to chatting, they bring me in whether they want to or not. Besides, who do you think put her up to her night with you?"

Now Lancer knew he'd been had by a very strong and cunning woman. He set down his empty glass carefully.

"You know, if you pour me another shot of that Napoleon, I'll raise a toast to you, Rosa," he said. "Remind me never to tangle with you."

"That might be a pleasure in itself, if Essie is to be believed."

Lancer blushed and began sipping the second drink. Rosa settled herself opposite him and proceeded to lay out an offer that could turn the tide against the Mannings. She said she could provide armed volunteers to help him in the coming battle.

"I can supply you with 20 men on horses and another dozen to place where you want them. They are good shots, and they are also very good with the machete," she said. "All they would ask is to be a part of the community when it's over. That's it."

The offer took the man in black by surprise, but he found it intriguing. The biggest potential sticking point was that he had no idea how Stoudenmire would react to it. The marshal represented a mostly white ruling class in El Paso, and they were paying his salary. Still, Stoudenmire understood that the time was coming when Mexicans were going to be a major part of the community. What better way to gain acceptance than a debt owed to save their skin. No question, this was a mighty interesting offer and at the same time a dilemma.

Lancer decided to play the middleman to buy time to think this through. "You present me with some options, Rosa. But I have to tell you Marshal Stoudenmire is running the show, so it will be up to him. I'll talk to him, but for now, let's keep it on the down low, so to speak. Now what about Essie?"

Rosa also was biding her time. She was going to play her cards in some fashion. She knew Stoudenmire would need to come back to her, because the Mannings had way too many friends. She got up and opened the door. Essie was coming down the stairway at that very moment. Their eyes met and Essie knew she was being summoned.

Essie entered the office and Rosa closed the door behind her. The young woman was startled to see Lancer standing in the room.

"What's he doing here?" she asked in an indignant tone.

"Don't worry, Essie," Rosa said reassuringly. "He's here to help."

"Help? Why would he help us? He's working for the marshal, and the marshal plans to kill James! Why is he here?"

Lancer moved away from the wall and into the middle of the room.

"The marshal doesn't plan on letting James die, Essie," he said confidently. "He wants to see him get a fair trial, that's all. If the judge hears the evidence and there is no trouble, we're all certain James will go free. The marshal wants to make sure, since the dead man is his brother-in-law, that there is no cover-up or undue influence involved. That's it."

Essie began to get teary-eyed. In another moment she collapsed in a chair, bawling her eyes out. Rosa came over to comfort the young woman. It had been a long time since she herself had been in love, but she remembered the feeling of love slipping out of her grasp.

Rosa offered a brandy in hopes of calming the girl. "Here, drink this."

Essie pushed it away, preferring to cry.

"Now, that's not a way to treat a fine brandy like that, Essie," Lancer said with a smile. "That bottle is older than you and me put together."

The comment accomplished what Lancer hoped it would. Essie smiled and realized the humor in it. First she smiled, then she began to laugh. Rosa hugged her and asked her to answer Lancer's questions because he had become a friend.

"What is it you want to know, Señor Lancer?"

He sat down in front of her and took her hands in his.

"Essie, have you had any conversations with the Mannings about their plans?"

"Not with Frank or Jeff. Only with James, and he doesn't tell me much," she said. "I don't think he knows much."

"Has he said anything, anything at all, about what they plan to do?"

"I know Frank is bringing in gunmen from all over the area," she said. "Bad men, men with a price on their head."

Lancer already knew this from his meeting with Rebo but it was good to hear someone confirming it. He continued to question Essie about her talks with James. Finally she came up with something he didn't know.

"One of the men is named Riley, and that seemed to be a cause for concern for Frank," she said. "James did say this Riley man is someone not to be trusted."

Lancer thought for a moment, and the anger in his eyes was obvious to Rosa.

"You know this Riley?" Rosa asked.

He nodded.

"Big Jay Riley, one of the worst to ever walk the planet," Lancer replied. "Would kill his own mother for a dollar and then shoot a hole in it to mock her death. He's a mean one."

Rosa did not look happy. Suddenly her thoughts turned to things that might go wrong and perhaps her having to face this Riley alone.

"Riley is the worst kind of killer there is," Lancer continued. "Kills for the fun of it. Gets a thrill out of someone else's death. We had an encounter up in Kansas City years ago. I should have killed him then, when I had the chance."

The two women were hanging on every word as Lancer went on with the story.

"He robbed a bank and killed the guard, a woman and a little boy." Lancer's anger began to grow. "By the time I showed up, he was holding the woman hostage. His ultimatum was if I pulled my gun, he'd kill her. Her little boy was lying wounded on the floor inside the bank. He said I could tend to the little boy and he'd ride out of town with the woman and let her go in an hour. It was all he wanted -- an hour."

"And you let him go," Essie said.

"I had no choice," Lancer replied. "If I shot, he'd certainly kill the woman, leaving the child without a mother. There was a chance the little boy would live if we got him to a doctor."

"The little boy died, didn't he?" Rosa asked with a tear welling up in her eye.

Lancer hung his head. "Before we could get him to the doctor."

"And his mother?" Essie queried.

"We found her dead alongside the road, a hundred yards outside of town. Her throat had been slit."

The two women were in tears and Lancer was close to it himself. It was the worst of the worst he'd ever faced, and there had been little he could do. His best effort to prevent tragedy had left two people dead and left a horrible killer on the loose to kill again.

"If we come face to face, there won't be a chance for Jay Riley to escape this time," Lancer said, smacking his fist on his gun belt for emphasis. "No, not this time."

"What about James?" Essie asked.

Lancer had almost forgotten about James Manning in his anger over Big Jay Riley. He went on to tell the women of his plan, after swearing them both to secrecy. By now Essie understood that if she had any hope of being with James Manning again, she needed to put her trust in Lancer. She did trust him, and in turn she wanted him to trust her by allowing her to visit James. Lancer agreed, thinking the Mannings would be less likely to get suspicious if she continued to act normally.

Back at the jail, Stoudenmire had been true to his word. When Lancer arrived, a dozen men were being sworn in as deputies. Among them were some who were good with a gun and a few who were not. Hart and Jessup Williams were both there, despite Jessup's desire to keep Hart out of the fight.

"Aren't you a little young to be in this fight, boy?" Lancer asked Hart.

Hart was indignant. He thought he'd demonstrated the necessary skills during the attack on the stagecoach, but he'd obviously missed something.

"I can shoot and I can plan and I think I proved both of those!"

"True, you did. But I don't want a kid like you out in the street," Lancer replied. "I need you back here in case they come for James. Someone who can keep a cool head needs to be here."

Hart realized he was being trusted and was actually getting a key assignment. Jessup leaned over to Lancer and gave him the smile only a father could give when he knew his son was being protected.

Stoudenmire interrupted with an announcement. "Men, this here is Lancer. He's going to be directing this shebang if it happens. I know him from the past and from the war. He's an expert in military strategy and that's what we need. Do what he tells you, every time he tells you, and we all might get out of this alive."

Lancer moved to the front of the crowd. As he addressed the men he tried to size them up. They were some in need of some training, and he didn't have time to train them. The offer from Rosa now seemed very attractive. He'd bring it up to Stoudenmire after the meeting. Tossing it in the faces of these townspeople was not going to be productive.

"Now, we don't know much about who is in the Manning crowd, except for a few names," he said. "We do know they are the worst scoundrels, with reputations of shooting straight and deadly. They might cause a diversion, they might go headlong into a full-on charge down the street. If we had more time or more names, we might get a clue on what to expect. Right now, I fear they may use a charge as a diversion to get to the jail."

A man in the back spoke up. It was the town barber, Jilly Buxton. Jilly had a good ear and Lancer's father had always told him if you wanted to get the pulse of the people, go to the local barbershop. It was always entertaining, if not informative.

"I heard a name," Buxton said. "A man named Gerber has joined them. Don't know much else. Jeff Manning mentioned it when I had him under the towel."

Lancer thought for a moment.

"Colonel Gilbert Gerber?"

"That sounds right," Jilly offered back.

"That is important. I know of his tactics," Lancer said. "That changes things. Men, I want you to all go home, get some rest, and we'll meet again tomorrow after the trial is adjourned for the day. I want a tight lid on this, so I'm not saying much now."

Several of the men began to grumble. What were they doing here if they couldn't be trusted? They walked out and Lancer pulled the marshal aside.

"I know Gerber from the war. Fought with him on more than one occasion," Lancer said. "Terrible strategist and even worse ethics. Looted several mansions along the Mississippi during one campaign. Heard several wagons went back to Michigan labeled as war supplies and ended up in a warehouse in his hometown." Stoudenmire listened thoughtfully.

Lancer went on to explain that Gerber always believed in a full frontal attack. He was known for it. Got a lot of boys killed that way, but felt to rush them through would scare the enemy into a retreat. That would make it easy to pick off the enemy soldiers as they ran. It worked, but the cost in lives was high. Colonel Gerber didn't believe in diversions and had no use for them.

Lancer now felt his side had an advantage. He and Stoudenmire would place men on the rooftops and in the windows of the upper floors, covering the entire center of town. When the gang came charging down the street, it would be met with a volley of rifle fire. The Manning gang would be stunned into retreat to regroup and try again. The second wave would deplete their numbers enough to hopefully make them think again.

Either way, leaving young Hart at the jailhouse should be enough. Lancer was convinced there would be no diversion tactic and the jail would be safe. He then impressed upon Stoudenmire the fact that Big Jay Riley was in the camp, and Riley might use the attack for his own diversion to pull off a robbery. Lancer knew Riley would also come gunning for him.

"My attentions will be divided once I spot Riley, so you will need to really take charge when that happens, my friend," Lancer said.

The marshal understood. "We'll get it done."

Lancer decided now was the time to bring up his ace in the hole. "Dallas, I got an offer from Rosa about another army we can use."

"Mexicans!"

"Yes, Mexicans," Lancer shot back. "Good guns, more than a dozen on horse and another dozen on the street."

"I'll rot in hell before I consent to using a Mexican army in any of my battles," Stoudenmire said defiantly. "The town fathers would hang me."

"If we lose this fight, the town fathers will be hanging themselves."

CHAPTER EIGHT

Colonel Gil Gerber graduated from West Point, but barely. He finished 99th in his class of 100. The only officer to graduate lower was killed a week before commencement when his horse threw him. To say Gerber was a lousy officer was just the start of it. No one liked him, which was why, when they decommissioned officers after the war, he was one of the first to go.

His record in battle as far as won and lost wasn't bad -- it was the way he achieved it. His belief in full frontal assaults got him the nickname of Bloody Gil. In one battle, he had a small Confederate force surrounded. He had plenty of time to wait them out. They were starving and low on ammunition. His scouts confirmed the enemy's position and plight.

Gerber waited two days, and when the Rebels still did not surrender, preferring to seek better terms, Gerber decided it was time to end the siege. If he'd have waited one more day, according to the Rebel officer in charge, they'd have taken the entire garrison without a shot being fired. The officer only wanted to make sure his men were going to be fed and the wounded were going to be treated well. Gerber wouldn't give a guarantee. It was surrender and then talk.

Bloody Gil sent 500 men on a full frontal charge up a hill manned by 100 Confederate riflemen. When the Rebs finally ran out of ammunition, 250 Union soldiers were dead and another 125 wounded, of which 30 would later die. In all 280 brave men and boys would find an early grave due to Gerber's foolishness. Another 95 would never be the same.

Gerber was one of two reasons Lancer chose to leave the U.S. Army. The other was Major General George Custer, who in his own way was no better than Gerber. Lancer served under Custer but resigned his commission just before the Little Big Horn. He'd probably have been with Reno, looking back, but either way he was not going to serve under a man with no regard for human life and devoted only to his own legacy and glory.

Bloody Gil left the Army too, and tried his hand as an Indian fighter, then trapper, and he even worked for the railroad for a time. None of those jobs suited him. Finally he started a security outfit, hiring out gunmen and offering advice to foreign powers as a military consultant. None of that worked out well for him. So it seemed only natural to Lancer that Gerber would join up with the Manning gang.

"Frank, as your chief strategist in this affair, I know only too well what you are facing and how to get this job done," Gerber said as he sat down to after-dinner drinks at the Manning Ranch. "I learned a lot in that bloody war, and well, sir, I'm looking forward to this battle."

Frank Manning was impressed with the colonel's credentials, as offered by the colonel himself. Frank had no reliable information, except from Gerber and a few of the hired men he'd brought with him.

"I want you to understand, Colonel," Frank said, "if my brother is set free, all of this is off. There will be no need for bloodshed. But if he's convicted, it's your show to run."

Gerber agreed with a nod. "Let's begin planning the siege of El Paso, shall we?"

Frank wasn't completely convinced he had a solid deal. This man struck him as a little too cocky to be trusted. But the former Union officer was being hired to do a job, and Frank felt he must let him do it.

The colonel began to lay out his plan. He reached into his vest and pulled out a crude map he'd drawn of the town, unfolding it on the dinner table. He pointed to the jail in the center of El Paso, where James was being held. The saloon was across the street. The bank was located halfway between the town's west entrance and the jail.

"Who did you say was running the show for the town?" he asked Frank.

"A man named Lancer," Jeff chimed in. "Friend of the marshal."

"Lancer... Lancer... ," Gerber repeated, trying to place the name. "Wait, Lancer out of Tombstone?"

Frank spoke first. "I think so. Right, Jeff?"

"Yes, goes by one name and works out of Tombstone," Jeff said. "Claims he's a friend of Wyatt Earp and Marshal Stoudenmire."

"Well, well, well," Gerber said. "I knew him during the war, but he wasn't Lancer then. Rich kid. Smart. Got himself a battlefield commission at Bull Run. Daddy couldn't pull enough strings for him to get into West Point like me. And then I had to work my way through. Him, he gets a commission on the field. Never should have happened."

Frank had to steer the colonel back to planning and leave his memories of Lancer alone. Gerber suddenly snapped his fingers.

"I got it! Lancer will never figure on this. We'll do the full frontal charge like I always did, but we'll use it as a diversion. Once we draw out the guns, and there can't be very many, we'll drop back and hit the jail to get your brother out. How does that sound?"

Frank smiled and looked at Jeff, who also broke into a smile.

"All right, then, that's how we'll do it," Gerber said, puffing out his chest. "Lancer will never know what hit him. Got any cigars around here? General Sherman never went into battle without one. Taught me all I know, he did."

Jeff brought over a small box from a table at the end of the room. He opened it and Gerber grabbed half a dozen of the Mannings' finest cigars. The brothers traded uncertain glances. Gerber caught that and laughed it off, putting five cigars in his coat pocket and holding the sixth up to wait for a light. Seeing this display of the colonel's arrogance made the Mannings vaguely wonder if this man was really on their side or merely his own.

So far the whole plan was looking shaky. They'd hired a colonel who hated Lancer and wanted to embarrass him at any cost; Big Jay Riley, whose biggest priority seemed to be killing Lancer; and a slew of ruthless gunmen who would shoot up a town, kill anyone for money and rape any woman in sight. Frank didn't like himself about now, but he vowed to get past it.

Jeff was having some of the same thoughts, but he was younger and enamored with the way of the gun. He would ask some of the boys to teach him the ropes. That would have to wait for another day, though. The trial was starting on the morrow.

Jeff walked outside and stood on the porch, surveying the vast Manning spread. He loved this place and didn't want to leave. But his impetuousness tugged at him too. He wanted to explore the area outside West Texas. He'd been listening to the tales of the gunmen his brother had hired and he was drawn in by their adventures in the wild West. Jeff looked out over the ranch with a full moon shining on the land. His daydream was interrupted by his brother, who had also stepped away from the meeting with Gerber to get some fresh air.

"Whatcha thinking about, little bro?"

Jeff kept looking out on the prairie and didn't turn around.

"Something wrong?"

"No, nothing. Do you think we're doing the right thing? I mean, hiring these killers?"

Frank handed one of their precious cigars to Jeff, who struck a match and lit it.

"I know we need to do something," Frank said. "I know what you mean, though. I'm wondering what Pa would do. I know he wouldn't let James hang, that's for sure."

Jeff nodded in agreement. "When this is all over," he said, "I'm going to leave here, head west, and see some things I've never seen before." Frank arched his eyebrows questioningly.

"Not that I'd be gone for good," Jeff added hurriedly. "A few years, maybe. You'd be welcome to my share, you know that."

Frank put his hand on his brother's shoulder to end the conversation. "Little brother, we'll talk about that when this is all over. But for right now we have -- what did the colonel call it -- 'a siege' to plan."

Frank turned and walked back into the house while Jeff stood outside, puffing thoughtfully on the cigar. Suddenly he held it out and looked at it with disdain, remembering he actually didn't like cigars that much. He tossed it into the dirt and walked off toward the stables. A late night ride might make him feel better about the colonel and his strategy, or at least help clear his mind.

CHAPTER NINE

Judge Blakemore was a good man, or tried to be. He'd served as a judge for 20 years and before that as a prosecutor in New Orleans. Before his prosecuting days, he was an attorney who hung out his own shingle in Baton Rouge. He was a man of the South, but his heart rang true to Union law. He fiercely opposed Jim Crow laws and hated the Klan. He had gained a reputation far and wide as a fair jurist, which was why Stoudenmire knew the Mannings had nothing to fear. When this judge ruled on the James Manning case, it would be a good ruling.

Stoudenmire himself had no ambitions beyond his duties in El Paso. He didn't want to run for higher office, and at this point in his life he was looking to settle down to a peaceful life in El Paso. He'd thought about moving to Mexico after his term was up, and he was ready to retire, but those thoughts were still in the distance. Well, maybe they were a little closer now that his brother-in-law was dead and his wife might want to put space between herself and El Paso. They had already talked about moving east anyway.

Truth be told, the marshal wasn't sure how he wanted the trial to end. He wanted justice for his wife and Doc Cummings and for the people of El Paso as well. When it came down to it, law and order was what he really wanted. If James Manning could have avoided killing a man, then he needed to pay for what he'd done. If Doc was at fault, Stoudenmire would grudgingly have to settle for an acquittal.

Stoudenmire's biggest concern was the stink the Mannings were making over this, and there wasn't even a trial yet. Since they'd already put together a private army of killers, there was going to be bloodshed if James was convicted. That was something Stoudenmire could not allow. And what if the judge said James was not guilty? Would this band of killers leave peacefully? He believed some would, but he knew some would not, and that would make things really tough for the citizens of El Paso. What if some of the killers decided to make El Paso "their" town? The possibilities made his head spin.

The jailhouse door opened and in walked Lancer with a dinner tray and a bottle.

"Whatcha got there?" Stoudenmire asked.

"A little dinner for both of us, and a drink to wash it down."

"I've already eaten dinner," Stoudenmire said, waving him off.

"Call it a late-night snack," Lancer replied. "Tomorrow's going to be a long day. You may not get breakfast, or at least you may not get to enjoy it."

The marshal understood and pushed aside the clutter so his desk could serve as a dinner table. Lancer had brought some tasty-looking food from Rosa's Cantina. A couple of small steaks, potatoes and gravy, biscuits and corn, and a side of apple pie.

"You call this a snack?" the marshal asked with a smile.

"Growing men are like growing boys," Lancer said. "And good food should never go to waste. Rosa sent me over with it. Said it was the end of the night and she had some extra food."

"Bless her little heart," Stoudenmire said as he reached over and took a quick bite of the pie. He smiled wide after tasting how good it was.

The two men sat down to eat and chatted about what was going to happen the next day. They discussed the best way to make sure James Manning made it safely from the jail to the courtroom. The men they'd hired would be served breakfast in the jailhouse, then quietly sent to their positions around seven in the morning. The trial would start at nine.

Judge Blakemore came by to pay his respects.

"You like apple pie, sir?" Lancer asked.

The judge answered with a broad smile. "Does a bear like honey?"

"Well, here, take my piece. I have my own dessert that I bring with me, so you go ahead and take the sweet pie."

"Don't mind if I do," the judge said. "But what's this favorite delicacy you speak of?"

Lancer walked over to his saddlebag hanging on the wall and took out his box of Turkish Delight. The judge had never heard of it. But the marshal was quite familiar with it. He'd shared Lancer's tasty treat since early in their friendship. Now it was the judge's turn to sample it. Then he sampled it again.

Lancer chuckled. "Well, you sure do have a sweet tooth, Your Honor."

"You haven't lived if you don't have a sweet tooth," Blakemore said, rubbing his hand on his ample belly. "And my wife isn't a bad cook, either."

Jeff Manning rode into town. His late-night ride had taken him farther than he'd intended, but now that he was here, he decided to visit his brother. He'd spent little time with James since the shooting, and thought he should make up for that. He rode up behind the jail and saw the light still on. He heard talking as he approached. Peering cautiously through a small window, he could see Lancer, Stoudenmire, and a distinguished-looking gent he assumed was Judge Blakemore.

Hidden from view in the dark, he decided to eavesdrop and see what he could learn. He heard Stoudenmire talking about men on the roof and in the buildings lining the street. He knew this was something Colonel Gerber would need to know. Frank's small army would be riding into a trap.

Lancer looked up and saw the tip of a hat barely visible in the corner of the window. Whoever was there didn't belong there and must be listening in but couldn't see them. Lancer motioned to Stoudenmire in the direction of the window and got up. He glided silently to the door, and the judge also caught on. Suddenly Lancer bolted out the door and came up right behind Jeff Manning with his gun drawn.

"Hands up!" Lancer exclaimed. Jeff did exactly as he was told.

"March yourself inside, and don't try anything."

Jeff willingly obliged. He knew he was trapped. He stepped through the door with his hands in the air to see a wide-eyed Marshal Stoudenmire and a confused-looking Judge Blakemore.

"Jeff Manning, well I declare, what the hell did you think you were you doing outside the jail?" Stoudenmire asked angrily.

"What did you hear, boy?" the judge demanded.

"Enough to know you won't get away with your stinkin' plan," Jeff sneered. "My brother and his men will tear this town apart before you gun them down. You'll see!"

Lancer prodded Jeff from behind, forcing him into a chair to face the three men.

"Look, young man, I promised your brother a fair trial, and that's what he'll get," Blakemore said. "If he's innocent, he'll go free, and if he's not, he'll pay the price."

"So, you might hang him!" Jeff shouted.

"Quite possible, yes. But don't put the cart in front of the horse here," the jurist answered. "Could be manslaughter, which would be jail time, or maybe even acquittal."

Stoudenmire leaned in toward Jeff. "That's right, boy. If Doc Cummings pulled first and it was self-defense, your brother will walk out of here clean as a whistle in time for dinner. Now you go on home."

Jeff looked up surprised. "You're letting me go?"

The marshal looked at Lancer. "Has he broken any laws?"

Lancer shook his head and turned to Blakemore. "Your Honor?"

"Can't say I know of any."

"Well then," Stoudenmire said to Jeff, "git out of my sight and don't come back. And tell that brother of yours we're ready if he comes."

Unnerved, Jeff got up and looked around the room. The marshal's personal assurance had given him hope the trial would actually be fair. He hurried out without saying a word. His thoughts would be reserved for Frank and the colonel. They needed to know.

The three men inside the marshal's office glanced at each other as if to say, "Okay, now what do we do?"

Stoudenmire looked deflated. "Our plan is blown wide open. They'll be ready for us. We just lost the element of surprise."

The judge was even more worried. He had the biggest decision to make and knew he had a target on his back. The marshal tried to ease his fears.

"Don't worry, Your Honor. We'll protect you. Don't let this whole thing change the way you judge this case. You need to be fair and true."

Looking harried, the judge poured himself a drink. And then another. Getting up, he headed for the door, then turned to face Stoudenmire and Lancer. "You men get this right and I'll get it right."

He walked out, leaving Lancer and the marshal wondering where he stood.

Lancer suddenly perked up. "I have an idea. I'll be back."

Stoudenmire tried to ask what that idea was, but Lancer, anticipating the question, shut him down quickly with just one word. "Rosa."

With that he left the jailhouse and Stoudenmire poured himself a drink. Tomorrow was going to be a long day.

On his way to Rosa's Cantina, Lancer noticed the light in the prosecutor's office was still lit. Henry Billings was working late. Lancer knocked on his door. Billings looked out the window to see who it was. He opened the door and Lancer came in.

"Mr. Lancer, to what do I owe the pleasure?"

"Oh, just moseying by and saw the light on," Lancer answered. "All set for the trial tomorrow?"

The lawyer sighed and shrugged. "As best as I can be. What's on your mind?"

Lancer walked slowly around the room for a moment before sitting down and putting his feet up on the prosecutor's desk.

"You know, something bothers me about this case, and I can't get it out of my mind."

"What's that?"

The lawyer sat down in another chair and Lancer removed his feet, realizing his manners were not too good at the moment.

"Two things, actually. First, do you believe Cummings was so drunk he could even reach for his weapon, let alone shoot straight? And second, I'm curious to know the position of Parsons when

Cummings pulled him by the arm. What could he have seen?"

The lawyer sat back and pondered the questions. "Both those things bother me as well. Doc was the only doctor in town. So any questions regarding how drunk is 'too drunk' would have to be answered by an out-of-town doctor, and while I tried, I was unable to get one here for the trial."

Lancer nodded.

"On the second matter, you've given me more room for thought," Billings said, looking toward the ceiling as if hoping to find an answer there. "I'll put some more effort into that one."

Lancer got up to leave. "Good. Just thought I'd get those things off my chest before this whole thing gets started. See you in the morning."

Billings ushered him to the door. "How's the security coming?"

Lancer smiled confidently. "We'll be ready for them, if they come."

CHAPTER TEN

To his credit, James Manning was up and ready to
go to trial well before he was served breakfast in
his jail cell. Coffee, eggs, bacon, biscuits and a
side of sweet jam were the morning offering.
When Dallas Stoudenmire opened the door
separating the cellblock from the outer office,
Manning could hear the sound of men talking in
low voices. He didn't know it yet, but these were
men hired to protect the judge and the integrity of
the law from his own brother's army.

"Here you go, young fella," Stoudenmire said
quietly as he slipped the food to Manning through
a slot in the cell door. "Have a hearty breakfast.
We'll be leaving within the hour."

Manning took the food and didn't say a word. As
the marshal left, Lancer stepped up to the cell door
to face Manning. "I'm here to discuss a few details
with you. You go ahead and munch on your
breakfast and I'll give you the details."

Lancer told him he would be escorted to the
courthouse in handcuffs by five armed men. James
scowled as he sat on his bunk and ate his breakfast.
He barely looked up and wasn't happy knowing he
would be going on trial shortly.

Lancer continued spelling out how the day would unfold. "You probably know your brother has hired some of the worst killers in the Southwest, in case things don't go well for you. You might want to try to talk him out of it."

James sat quietly for a moment, then shrugged and shook his head to dismiss the idea.

Lancer wasn't going to take no for an answer and raised his voice for emphasis. "Look, a man is dead and usually unless it's totally witnessed as self-defense, someone has to pay for the man's killing. There's a good chance you'll have to do some time. The people of this town should not have to pay if that happens. They didn't kill Doc Cummings. You did."

James shot up angrily from his bunk, spilling what was left of his food on the cell floor. He charged over to the bars and faced Lancer.

"Yes, a man's dead, a man who pulled a gun. Now maybe I could have waited and maybe I'd be the one lying out there in a wooden box. But he's dead and I'm not, and I don't deserve to die or spend years in prison for it!"

He turned around and stared out the cell window before turning back to Lancer.

"Those people out there don't give a damn about Doc Cummings," he shouted. "They only care a Manning is going to pay for his killin'. They either hate us or love us, and those that love us want something from Frank and me. So I don't give a damn about your precious El Paso people and I don't give a damn if Frank rips this town apart. I'm the one who's gonna pay if your precious judge decides wrong. Me! Not them!"

With that he sat down hard on the bunk. Marshal Stoudenmire, hearing the commotion, came running in.

"Get him out of here and leave me alone!" Manning yelled as the conversation in the office dropped to a low hush.

Lancer and the marshal walked out, closing the door behind them. Feeling utterly powerless, Manning wept.

The entire town turned out for the trial, and it was standing room only in the back of the courtroom. The gallery above was also packed. The overflow spilled into the next room. The day was warm, so the courtroom windows were open and people huddled around them to listen from the outside. Unbeknownst to the spectators, men with rifles and shotguns were taking up positions nearby to thwart the potential attack by the Manning gang. Lancer placed some of his riflemen on the rooftops as planned. Others were hidden behind second-story windows or inside buildings such as the stables.

Lancer wasn't too worried this early in the day because it wasn't likely Colonel Gerber and Frank Manning were going to order an attack until after the trial. He knew Gerber's men were waiting a few miles outside of town. He'd sent Hart out there to scout, and the young man had come back with some good information. In all, there were about 30 gunslingers, including the colonel.

Lancer assigned himself to be inside the courtroom, but off to the side with easy access out. The place was loud when the bailiff announced Judge Blakemore's entrance: "All rise!" Everyone stopped talking and stood up. The black-robed judge seated himself and rapped his gavel twice. "In the matter of The People of El Paso versus James Manning, this court is now in session. Mr. Manning, you are charged with the murder of a citizen of El Paso, Doc Cummings. Mr. Prosecutor, please outline your case.

Henry Billings began his opening statement. "Your Honor, we will tell the tale of how an angry man gunned down a prominent citizen of this town in cold blood. Even though the deceased, Doc Cummings, was armed, his gun was still in his holster when he was found dead on the street outside the local saloon. His gun never cleared leather."

At that moment, James Manning leaped defiantly from his chair. "That's a lie! That's a lie!!"

The crowd went crazy and the judge moved to restore order by banging his gavel several times. Defense attorney Solomon Archer grabbed Manning by the shoulders and pulled him back to his seat.

"Counselor, control your client or I'll have him removed from this court!" Judge Blakemore declared.

Archer, realizing that things had just gotten off to a bad start, immediately tried to smooth things over. "We apologize for the interruption, Your Honor." Blakemore nodded sternly and sat back in his chair.

Archer had been brought in from Abilene to defend Manning and was known as an astute attorney. He'd spent much of his time in St. Louis before moving to Texas. He thought that it would be a good place to make a name for himself, having heard that justice was being administered haphazardly. But when he arrived in Texas, he discovered it wasn't as wild as he'd heard. But he stayed, figuring the state was in need of a good and decent defense attorney.

He'd once gotten a man off for shooting another man in the back. A posse had been ready to hang the accused right after the shooting, but a local judge ordered a trial. Archer proved the dead man had been reaching for a gun while turning his back when he was shot and killed. It didn't help the deceased man's cause that he was in bed with the killer's wife when the shooting took place. That swayed the jury in favor of Archer's client, and he got the man an acquittal. James Manning was hoping for the same. Archer had seemed confident of a favorable outcome when James talked to him in jail.

Henry Billings was a lifelong El Paso citizen, and third generation as well. His father was a lawyer before him, and it fell to young Henry to carry on the family business. No one challenged him when he ran for city prosecutor. He gained a reputation for being tough but fair -- and relentless in going after criminals. And everyone knew he was no friend of the Manning clan.

While there was a parade of witnesses to testify that Doc Cummings was in the saloon that fatal night, there was just one key witness. Bill Parsons was the only person who saw the shooting, besides James Manning. And Doc Cummings, who of course would not be testifying. Stoudenmire had already testified that Doc's gun was still holstered when he was found dead. As a lawman, his words held great sway with the court.

Frank and Jeff Manning sat quietly behind their brother in the courtroom, neither saying a word.

"Mr. Bill Parsons, please step to the witness stand," the bailiff instructed.

Parsons slowly moved from the back of the room to the witness stand next to the judge. He took the oath to tell the truth and sat down.

"State your name for the record," the judge ordered.

"My name is William Parsons, but most people call me Bill. Your Honor, you can call me Bill."

Everyone in the courtroom laughed and Parsons shrank a bit in his chair. He wasn't accustomed to being the center of attention. Known mainly for being the town drunk, he was well aware that everyone laughed at him behind his back, and some in front of him. But he wasn't expecting that treatment in a formal setting like this.

The judge felt a little bad for him and said in a kind tone, "Mr. Parsons, just answer the questions the best you know how."

Archer's questions took the man slowly through what he saw that night. Parsons told how Doc had obviously been drinking and was stumbling near the saloon when he encountered James Manning. Neither man budged when they met.

"They were both stubborn as mules, they were," Parsons testified. "A real pair of jackasses if you ask me."

The men in the courtroom laughed again. Parsons was getting more attention than he'd ever had and now he was actually enjoying it.

"So, Mr. Parsons," Archer continued, "when Mr. Cummings grabbed your arm, what did you see next?"

"Well, he put me between the two of them and then he reached for his gun. But James Manning was much quicker on the draw and he fired. Doc was dead in the wink of an eye. Doc was drunk, but he pulled first."

"Your Honor, the defense rests," Archer announced with an air of victory.

Half the crowd sat in stony silence while the other half erupted in cheers. James was smiling. From their front-row seats, Frank and Jeff reached across the rail and gave their brother congratulatory pats on the back.

Now it was the prosecutor's turn. Billings stood in front of the judge and looked at Parsons. He began with simple questions. "Where were you on the night Doc Cummings was killed?... Did you have much to drink that night?... Did you see both men clearly?"

Lancer stood off to the side, keeping a watchful eye but also marveling at the way Billings was putting Parsons at ease. Billings obviously didn't want to spook the man before hitting him with the tough questions. The biggest one would be: Did Doc pull his gun, or intend to?

The questions turned a little more intense. "Mr. Parsons," Billings said, "could you describe for the court the position you were in when you saw James Manning pull the trigger and kill Doc Cummings?"

Parsons thought for a moment and then said he could. Billings asked him to show the court physically where he was in relation to Doc and James.

"Right here? You want me to get up?"

The audience chuckled and Billings cleared his throat before nodding yes.

Parsons got up and described how he was caught between the two men, and then how Doc grabbed him as he tried to walk away.

"Which way were your facing then?" Billings asked.

The entire courtroom was quiet and listening to every word. If Parsons didn't already know where Billings was going, the audience did.

"Well, I was facing James when he pulled his gun." Parsons suddenly stopped as he realized he never saw Doc's hand and could not be sure if Doc did indeed pull his weapon.

"So, Mr. Parsons, it is your testimony that you never actually saw Mr. Cummings pull or not pull his weapon, because your back was turned when he supposedly would have taken that action?"

Parsons' shoulders sagged and he fell silent with the realization that his earlier conclusion had been fatally flawed.

"Mr. Parsons?" Billings prompted.

"Mr. Parsons, please answer the question," the judge ordered.

Parsons looked up at the judge and muttered, "No, I never saw Doc pull his gun."

Now it was the other half of the courtroom's turn to go wild. James Manning sat calmly in his chair. The judge pounded his gavel over and over until the crowd came to order. He told Parsons to step down. Head hung low, Parsons trudged out the door and headed down the street to the saloon, where he could drown his embarrassment in liquor.

The prosecutor rested his case and summed it up for the judge. "Your honor this was a case of pure murder and not self-defense at all," Billings said. "Mr. Cummings was too drunk to pull a gun. There is no evidence he even tried to pull his weapon, let alone that he pulled it. And if he *had* pulled it, there was no way he could have killed James Manning."

He paused before driving his point home. "If Mr. Manning had been so concerned, he could have disarmed Doc Cummings with his hands, or at worst shot and wounded him. No, instead he shot him point-blank and killed him. This was murder, Your Honor, and while there is some evidence of a grudge between the two, we won't even go there. We know there has been bad blood between

Marshal Stoudenmire, the brother-in-law of the dead man, and the Manning family. Even tossing that out as circumstantial, this is a case of murder. We ask the court to render a verdict of guilty."

Once again, half the courtroom cheered. Archer rose to sum up his case.

"Your Honor, the prosecutor may be correct on the action Mr. Manning *could* have taken. But the fact is, he saw a man pull a gun in front of him and reacted as any man would -- he pulled his own gun to defend himself and fired directly at the threat. The fact the bullet found its mark and did not wound Doc Cummings should be not even considered. Your Honor, this was a case of self-defense. We asked the court to render a *not* guilty verdict."

The judge nodded and sat up in his chair. "I'll take this under advisement and will issue my ruling tomorrow morning. This court is adjourned." Blakemore rapped his gavel and left. The courtroom began to clear out.

Marshal Stoudenmire, with Lancer at his back, moved James Manning out of the courtroom and down the street to the jail. There was no trouble, but a lot of folks were watching their own backs in the split town of El Paso.

As people were still leaving the courtroom, Frank Manning approached the marshal and gave him a warning. "You make sure my brother stays well tonight, because we're coming in the morning, should anything happen to him."

"He'll be fine, and if you try anything, Frank, he'll be the first to catch a bullet," Stoudenmire replied sternly. "You never know where a bullet may come from, now, do you?"

Frank clenched a fist and moved menacingly toward the marshal, but Lancer stepped between them. Not another word was said, but Lancer knew this display of bad blood only made his job tougher. He motioned to Frank to get on his horse, and Frank did so but grudgingly. He never took his eyes off Stoudenmire, and if eyes were bullets, the marshal would be lying in his grave.

That night was a long one for everyone involved. The citizens of El Paso talked about the day's testimony into the wee hours. The men hired by Stoudenmire whiled away the evening at the saloon. Lancer and the marshal took turns at keeping watch. James Manning paced the night away. Essie cried all night in Rosa's arms.

Judge Blakemore had it the roughest. Holed up in a hotel room under armed guard, he had a decision to make. The jurist pored over his lawbooks, looking for something, anything, he could find to make his decision easier.

As the night wore on, it was Lancer's turn to make the rounds in town and make sure no surprises were about to happen. He needed some fresh air, and a drink wasn't out of the question. He gave the marshal the high sign with his thumb and Stoudenmire followed him to the door, throwing the double bolt after Lancer walked out.

Lancer walked the main street of El Paso and imagined what Wyatt and Virgil went through every night as they did the rounds in Tombstone. He hadn't heard from his friends after the gunfight at the O-K Corral, but he knew he'd soon be back in Tombstone to hear the tale of what happened from a dozen or more folks who witnessed it, and some who said they did but weren't even in town that day. It always happened that way.

Just like Parsons' testimony, he thought to himself. Parsons believed he knew what he saw, but in reality he didn't see anything. It was partially instinct and partially wanting to be where you were not.

He checked a few doors and wandered over to the saloon. From outside, he heard some commotion behind the swinging doors. He decided to stand and listen before walking in.

He heard the loud voice of Big Jay Riley wafting through the doorway. "Now, we all know this judge is going to condemn James Manning when James isn't even guilty. The judge is on the side of the law, and we all know the law in this town is Dallas Stoudenmire, the brother-in-law of the dead man." Riley was whipping up a crowd of half-drunk men.

"And we all know what that means," he continued. "Now, we're riding into town tomorrow with 30 guns, and anyone who stands in our way is gonna get hurt. If you're sticking with the marshal, then you need to stop and think – where am I gonna lay my head tomorrow night? In my bed or on boot hill?"

Lancer had heard enough. He stepped through the swinging doors. The men stopped looking at Riley and swung their gaze to Lancer.

"Stop right there, Riley!" Lancer ordered.

Riley turned around to see his nemesis

"Well if it ain't the famous Lancer," Riley said with a smirk on his face. "I don't see no badge on you, so who are you ordering to stop anything?"

"I don't need a badge," Lancer said. "I'm here working for the marshal at his behest, and I'm ordering you to stop whipping these men into a frenzy. You say you're riding in with 30 guns, and that's law-breaking enough."

Riley squared off against Lancer. "I see you're wearing the big iron. How many men have you killed?"

"I don't keep track of such things."

"I know how many I killed," Riley said. "I got 20 notches on this gun, and room for 21."

Lancer stood still. He didn't want to fight right now. Too many people in the line of fire. Riley's hand was inching closer to his gun handle. Suddenly Riley heard a loud click behind him and he froze. Jessup Williams had a shotgun pointed at Riley's back and stood just two feet away.

"And my shotgun is itching for a notch right now, Riley," Williams said. "So unless you don't want to be that notch, you better lower your hand and move on."

Riley didn't have much choice. He backed away toward the door. Lancer turned with him as Williams followed. Riley pointed a finger as if it were a gun and aimed it right at Williams and Lancer.

"Bang bang on the morrow, gentlemen! Bang bang!" Riley warned before disappearing into the darkness.

Lancer and Williams both breathed heavy sighs over the trouble that had just been avoided, at least temporarily. Lancer turned to face the crowd of inebriated men.

"I have a few words for you fellas here in the saloon who listened to that nonsense from Big Jay Riley. Yes, they have 30 guns. But if we stick together, they won't take this town. Now, I can't promise you that you'll still be alive by the end of tomorrow. But I can promise you that if they come, and we resist, they will not win. Don't be scared off by Riley. He was sent here to lower the odds. Those of you who are with us, report to the jailhouse at seven tomorrow."

Some men grumbled and others turned toward the bar.

"For right now, the drinks are on me!" Lancer shouted to the bartender. "Just one each, though. Can't afford to let you men get too liquored up!"

Good-natured whoops and laughter broke out as the men headed over to the bar. Lancer pulled Jessup Williams aside.

"We'll need someone to stay back at the jail when the shootin' starts, to make sure they don't get to Manning," he said in an undertone. "Think your boy can handle it? I don't want him in the street when this all comes down."

"He'll handle it," Williams promised. "You can count on it."

CHAPTER ELEVEN

Hart Williams arrived early at the jail, much sooner than he needed to. By the time the men started filing into the office for breakfast at seven, Hart had been there an hour, had downed his breakfast of coffee and eggs, and was patrolling the outside of the jail with his musket in hand.

Marshal Stoudenmire marveled at the young man's diligence and poise. "You know, Lancer, this kid has the makings of a fine lawman."

"I think you are right, Dallas."

Jerry Rinter and Toe Slavin, two of the men Stoudenmire had hired to protect the town, came in together and did not look happy. They laid down their rifles on the desk in front of the marshal.

"What's this?" Stoudenmire asked blankly.

"We're out. It's too dangerous," Rinter said. Slavin nodded in agreement. "We discussed it last night with our wives, after Riley made his speech. And well, we're family men, storekeepers. We're not lawmen. Keeping the peace isn't up to us."

Lancer picked up one of the rifles. "Not up to you? Well, I declare, was it up to the men at the Alamo? Concord? Lexington? How about the men who fought in every small town in history to protect their families? Was it up to them?"

Rinter stood silent but Slavin spoke up. "Those were different times, Mr. Lancer." He pointed to the holster with the crossed lances. And it's easy for you -- you carry a gun as your profession. Us? Like my friend said, we're just storekeepers. We've rarely ever fired a gun, let alone killed anyone."

The marshal was annoyed to hear this. "Oh c'mon, men, it's a little late for this!"

Lancer paced thoughtfully around the room for a moment. "What if the citizens of every small town along the Mississippi decided they were farmers and it was up to the Army to fight off the Indians who attacked their farms? Sure, the Army could do the job. But the military can only stay for so long. Then what? You have to step up and defend your own, even if it means you could lose your life."

Several of the other men came to Lancer's defense and urged the two men to stay on. But several others joined the pair's cause and decided to bail on the marshal's plan.

"I'm sorry, Mr. Lancer, Marshal, but I can't do it," Rinter said, hanging his head. "I have to go."

Stoudenmire stepped forward. "If there are any others here who are with these two men, then go now. No one will begrudge you that. You are not to be called cowards, but I'll take as many brave men as I can."

Half of the group quietly shuffled out, leaving only 10 gunmen to defend the town. The marshal was disappointed by this turn of events. Lancer went over to where he sat and put his hand on Stoudenmire's shoulder. "Gideon did more with less."

"Huh?" Stoudenmire asked, forgetting his Bible verses.

"When Gideon started out, he had 30,000 warriors. But the Lord said it was too many. And the Lord spoke to Gideon and said 'I will deliver you with the 300 men who lapped and will give the Midianites into your hands; so let all the other people go, each man to his home.' So the 300 men took the people's provisions and their trumpets into their hands."

Stoudenmire looked at him for a moment in sudden recollection. "And the Lord delivered them into his hands based on trumpets and confusion."

Lancer smiled. "Yes. And we have something Gideon did not – a courageous group of Mexicans."

As Lancer walked away, the marshal marveled at the wisdom of the man he'd brought to El Paso. He had truly made the right decision.

With breakfast over, Lancer ordered the riflemen to their spots on the rooftops. They would be spread out and difficult to find, if and when the shooting started.

Outside town, Frank and Jeff Manning were on horseback at the head of their band of killers. Rebo was there with them, but not as a fighter. His assignment was to make sure James Manning made it home.

Lancer walked across the street and saw Rosa standing on a corner not far away. She was disguised as an old Mexican woman, covered with a shawl. She nodded when she made eye contact with Lancer, then turned and left.

"C'mon, it's time," Stoudenmire said curtly to James Manning as he opened the cell door.

Hart Williams was standing nearby with his musket. Manning laughed but he felt a little sad, too. He knew the boy's life wouldn't be worth a dime if his brother came with the hired guns to set him free.

As they marched across the street with an armed guard, Stoudenmire saw the Manning brothers ride up casually to the courthouse. They got off their horses and met their brother.

"You okay?" Frank said to James.

James nodded.

"Don't worry, they are *not* going to hang you!"

"I hope we don't have to," Stoudenmire said to Frank. "You may not want to believe it, but I hope he goes free."

Frank spit on the ground in disgust, and so did Jeff. James didn't like that sign of disrespect but said nothing. They all moved into the packed courtroom. When the bailiff called for order, the judge entered and sat down. A hush settled over the room

"In the matter of the People of El Paso versus James Manning," Judge Blakemore began, "the court has undertaken all the testimony and all the words spoken yesterday and has come to a decision. I have searched all the lawbooks, and while it was not an easy case to decide, it is rather direct in its approach. I have complete confidence in my decision, which I shall render here and now."

Each person in the courtroom hung on every word the jurist was saying. Lancer stood in his place at the side door. He kept particular watch on Frank and Jeff Manning. If they pulled, he would have no choice but to pull as well, and his aim would be deadly.

"In looking over the evidence in the matter, there is no mistaking a man is dead. But as to whether or not it was murder, that is a different matter," Judge Blakemore continued. "It is clear Mr. Cummings was drunk, and it is clear Mr. Manning was not -- he had all his wits about him. If in danger, a citizen has the first responsibility to defend himself, but at the same time must take into account human life and the likely outcome of his actions. It is evident Mr. Cummings was in no shape to fire his weapon and endanger the life of James Manning. Mr. Manning had a responsibility to take a less lethal approach to the matter."

Frank and Jeff leaned their heads together. "He's going for guilty," Jeff whispered.

"Therefore," the judge continued, "I find the defendant *not* guilty of murder, but…."

The courtroom erupted but the Manning brothers stayed quiet because they could sense the judge had more to say.

The judge banged his gavel.

"Wait, wait, I'm not finished," he said as everyone quieted down. "While not guilty of murder, I find the defendant, James Manning, guilty of manslaughter."

The crowd again erupted. James Manning fell back in his chair, and while Archer tried to comfort him, Frank yelled at the judge. "Fraud! Fraud!"

Lancer moved over between the judge and the Mannings and fired a single shot into the ceiling. "Quiet! Let the man finish!"

The judge continued reading.

"Therefore I sentence James Manning to nine years in the state prison, but two of those are suspended and he will be eligible for parole in three years. This case is closed." The judge banged his gavel once, got up and hurried out the back door. Jessup Williams was waiting to escort him to the local stage, which was ready to take him out of town in a hurry. The stage would head east, avoiding the Manning gang at the west end of town.

Frank Manning confronted the marshal and shook a finger in his face. "You've just signed your death warrant and the death warrant of this town!" he said angrily. "This isn't over by any means." Turning to his brother, he said, "James, we'll get you out!"

"Frank, I can do three years, honest! Don't do something rash," James pleaded.

Frank was momentarily stunned by his brother's willingness to surrender his fate. He quickly decided it didn't matter. Plans had been put in motion and there was blood to shed. Jeff and Frank left the building and rode quickly out of town. Stoudenmire moved swiftly as well, taking James to the jailhouse. Hart Williams was ready and waiting.

As he watched the Manning brothers ride out of town, Lancer's mind roamed over the defenses. He knew where all of his men were, and they knew the plan. When Manning's army rode into town, the town defenders were to wait until the gang passed the third building and then they would open fire, taking out as many as possible in the first charge. That would cut the odds. Then they were to fall back to secondary positions, so when the second charge came they could fire with a surprise volley.

Outside of town, an angry Frank Manning addressed Colonel Gerber and his horde.

"Do your damndest, Colonel!" he shouted. "Tear that town apart if you have to. I'll work around you to get my brother out."

"Will do," Gerber said with a salute. "Men, let's go!"

Gerber led his 30 guns to the edge of town, where they pulled up to survey the situation. El Paso was quiet. There wasn't soul on the streets. He delayed long enough for Frank and Jeff Manning to get into position. Rebo sat at the rear of the gang, waiting and watching. He hated what he was seeing, but he didn't see any way out.

Lancer waited tensely across the street from the jail. Stoudenmire was positioned inside the saloon, while young Hart Williams stood alone in the jail, keeping a close eye on James Manning.

Then came the word from Colonel Gerber. "Charge!"

The killer gang, guns blazing, rushed headlong into El Paso. Shots blasted through shop windows as citizens ducked down behind anything they could use for cover. In the main saloon, every man hid behind an overturned table or the bar. Stoudenmire watched cautiously from one of the saloon's windows.

When the gangsters reached the third building into town, a volley of thunder came their way. Seven of them fell dead on the street. Two more were wounded. It was enough to secure Frank Manning's passage to the rear of the jail. Gerber's riders withdrew quickly. They had done their job. They reassembled for a second charge, not realizing the next volley would come at them from a different vantage point.

As Frank and Jeff Manning entered the back door of the jail, they saw Hart holding his musket on their brother. But the element of surprise was on their side. While Lancer and Stoudenmire repositioned their riflemen outside, Frank confronted Hart. "Drop the musket, boy!"

Hart was as scared as he was shocked. He realized he had failed but he decided to put up a brave front anyway. "I won't drop my weapon," he said defiantly.

"Son," Jeff warned him, "this ain't worth dying for. You got your whole life ahead of you, and we are going to get my brother out of here, even if it means over your dead body. Now step aside and hand me the keys."

Hart stood his ground.

"Give me the damn keys, kid!"

Hart knew it was a lost battle. He had been caught off-guard and he had no choice. He dropped his weapon and held out the keys. Jeff grabbed the musket and tossed it aside before taking the keys and letting his brother out of the cell.

James felt conflicted about turning into a jailbreaker. But hearing the gunfire outside persuaded him that his big brother was doing what he thought best. He grabbed his hat and gun off the wall and the three brothers raced out of the building.

Without thinking ahead, Hart grabbed his musket and gave chase. He knew he should let Lancer know about the jailbreak, but he was determined to make up for his failure. As the brothers climbed onto their horses, he raised his musket.

"Stop or I'll shoot!" he yelled.

Frank took no pity. He pulled his weapon and fired, hitting Hart in the chest, but not before the boy got off a shot himself. The musket ball found its way to the forehead of Jeff Manning, killing him instantly.

"No!!!" James yelled as Frank whirled around and saw his mortally wounded brother. Frank raised his pistol and fired at the boy again, but James knocked him off balance and the bullet landed harmlessly in the dirt.

"He's already dead! Enough!" James shouted. "Let's get Jeff and get out of here."

Jeff was still slumped on his horse as Frank took the reins and they fled. Stoudenmire, hearing the shots, ran from his position in the saloon to the back of the jail and saw them riding away. He fired three shots. James felt a bullet go deep in his chest. He stayed on his horse but he knew he was seriously wounded.

The Manning brothers rode on to the safety of the Gerber gang.

"Mr. Manning, what happened?" Gerber asked anxiously.

"My brother Jeff is dead, and James is hit," Frank yelled in anger. "Burn it! Burn the town! Leave Stoudenmire to me!"

Riley jumped in with his gun pulled. "And leave Lancer to me!"

Gerber ordered his men to charge in two waves. The first rode directly into the second volley, which didn't do as much damage as the first. The second wave came right behind, and now the riders knew where the riflemen were. They dismounted and went after the riflemen on foot. Several of the town's protectors beat a hasty retreat.

The Manning brothers were riding hard and fast back to their ranch. Rebo, seeing Jeff's lifeless body, began to weep. "Mister Jeff, he dead, sir, now why you have to go and do that?" He looked at Frank.

Frank's fury was turning into helplessness as he realized he needed to do something fast to save his brother James. "Rebo, you ride to fetch somebody who knows something about doctoring!"

"Ain't no doctor in El Paso now that Doc Cummings is dead," Rebo said. "You know that!" Frank understood all too well.

"Somebody there knows something," he yelled. "If you have to ride to Juarez, get me a Mexican doctor. Now go!"

Rebo took off toward the border. He knew if he didn't move, James would soon be joining Jeff in the cemetery.

As Gerber's men started to get the upper hand, it was time for Lancer to play his hand. He fired at the bell on top of the stable. It rang out loudly and the doors to the stable flew open. Out charged 25 Mexican horsemen, followed by another 25 men on foot with guns and machetes. The battle quickly turned.

The Mexicans battled hard, as if they were fighting for their own town. In essence they were. They were fighting for respect, the respect of the white citizens of El Paso who now would have to recognize their contribution to the safety of the town.

Gunshots flew. A rider on a horse was taken down by a man wielding a machete. He would never get up again. Bullets found their marks in rapid succession. Gerber, seeing the battle would be lost, turned and rode east through town to make a getaway.

Gerber had no chance to react to the shot that rang out as he passed Rosa's Cantina. The colonel fell dead in the street. Rosa herself had fired the fatal bullet.

Seeing the colonel tumble from his horse, Lancer quickly made his way to Rosa's. Stoudenmire was in charge of the battle now.

A mile outside of town, James Manning pulled up his reins. "I can't, Frank. I can't go on."

"C'mon, boy, it's not that far," Frank urged. "We'll get you fixed up at the ranch."

"I can't make it that far. I gotta see Essie. Thanks, Frank, but good-bye."

With that the middle Manning brother turned his horse around and rode as fast as he could toward town. He had to see his Essie one more time, for he knew she loved him and it drove him onward.

Reaching the outskirts of the city, he could see the battle raging. It was chaos and there was no way he'd make it to Rosa's Cantina. Weary and exhausted from the loss of blood, he turned his horse into the back alleys to make it to the back door of Rosa's. He was barely conscious when he got there and knew his time was short.

He staggered through the back door and into the main room. There stood Rosa, Essie and Lancer, who drew his gun. There was no need for it. He could see the man was seriously wounded and had only a few moments of life left in him.

Essie ran to her love. As he fell into her arms, she fell to her knees, holding him and looking down at his face.

"I love you Essie. I love you with all my heart," he whispered. "Kiss me one more time."

With tears in her eyes Essie leaned over his failing and bloody body and gave him a final kiss.

"Good-bye my love, good-bye," she said softly as her tears fell on his face, and then he was gone.

Rosa and Lancer stood over the pair. Rosa was weeping and Lancer could not speak. The love these two shared had been all but forgotten in the wave of hate that had filled the town. From the Mannings to the lawman who had a grudge against the man who now lay dead on the floor, it was the kind of hate that shatters lives forever. It was Stoudenmire's shot that had taken James Manning's life, and the marshal would have to live with that.

Behind the jailhouse, Jessup Williams suddenly spotted the nearly lifeless body of young Hart. He ran to the boy, who barely had any breath left in his lungs.

"Pa, I failed. I failed but I got one of them."

"Shhh, quiet now boy, don't speak," the father said, trying to hold back tears.

"I'm sorry, Pa."

"No son, you didn't fail, you done good," Jessup whispered. "We got them, all of them, and you did your part."

"That's good, right?" the boy asked with his final breath as his father held him close and sobbed.

The battle came to a close with the Mexicans, a few of Stoudenmire's riflemen and the marshal himself standing guard over all but one of the survivors of Manning's ill-fated brigade. The only one not there was Big Jay Riley. He was making his way toward Rosa's.

Lancer stood inside the cantina, looking down at the dead body of the man at the center of all that had happened. Suddenly he heard a voice from outside.

"Lancer!" Riley yelled. "It's you and me now!"

"Don't go out there" Rosa pleaded. "He'll kill you."

"This isn't the first time I've heard someone tell me that," Lancer replied.

The man in black checked the bullets in his gun and loaded what he needed. He glanced at himself in the mirror above the bar as he poured himself a whiskey.

"Lancer, I know you're in there!" Riley said menacingly.

Lancer calmly downed the whiskey as a crowd gathered outside. He turned and slowly walked out the door.

"You got a beef with me, Riley?"

"I see you got that big iron on your hip. How many men you killed with that thing?"

Lancer straightened his gun belt before replying. "I never count," he said evenly. "Seems like a waste of time."

Riley moved around to get a better position.

"Well I got 20 notches on my gun and room for 21," Riley reminded him with a crooked smile.

Lancer looked Riley straight in the eye and didn't blink.

"No, I think 20 is enough."

Riley paused. For the first time in years, he had second thoughts about a gunfight. Lancer could be faster and shoot straighter. Lancer could be right. This could be his last rodeo. He tried to shake off his doubts by showing bravado.

"No matter," he answered. "What's it to men like us? We all gotta go sometime."

The two men stared each other down, each waiting for the other to make a slip, a move, a twitch, anything to justify a response with a bullet.

It was Riley who moved first, but before his gun barrel saw sunlight, Lancer pulled his own gun and opened fire, hitting Riley in the heart. In that split-second while Lancer's bullet was plowing through his chest, Riley was able to get off a shot, but his bullet dove harmlessly into the ground between the two men. He stood there frozen for a moment and collapsed dead in the dusty street.

Lancer looked around and saw Stoudenmire in the crowd, watching and waiting to see what would come next. Lancer surveyed the rest of the spectators, then holstered his gun. He saw Slavin heading toward him, leading Lincoln. When Slavin handed over the reins, Lancer nodded his thanks.

He patted the great horse and hoisted himself into the saddle. The townfolk watched him ride calmly out of El Paso. He looked neither left nor right, except to glance at Rosa as he passed her. He smiled and tipped his hat to her in gratitude.

He was heading back to Tombstone, where he'd catch up on the tale of Wyatt and the Earp clan and see what might be in the offing. He'd be getting a telegram when he arrived. Javy would bring it to him. It would be from someone in need of his services in New Orleans.

He'd get another telegram before he left for New Orleans. It would be from Billings in El Paso, informing him Marshal Dallas Stoudenmire was dead. The only Manning still alive, Frank, came back to get revenge. Stoudenmire was drunk when he challenged Frank outside the saloon. Manning shot and killed him.

Frank Manning stood trial for the killing. But this time a jury made up mostly of his friends acquitted him. Judge Blakemore's body was found six months later, his throat slashed in a back alley. It was said he was killed by a Mexican in a robbery. Blakemore had $100 on him when his body was discovered. He also had on him a newspaper clipping that was stuffed in his jacket pocket. It told of the deaths of James and Jeff Manning and the battle of El Paso.

The killer was never found.

This is the fourth installment in the "Lancer; Hero of the West" series. You can find the others on Amazon, or you can find all of Bob Brill's books on www.bobbrillbooks.com. You can also order them wherever fine books are sold. You can also read about Lancer at the blog www.lancerheroofthewest.blogspot.com.

Lancer: Hero of the West – The Prescott Affair

Lancer: Hero of the West – The Los Angeles Affair

Lancer: Hero of the West – The Santa Fe Affair

Lancer: Hero of the West – The El Paso Affair

Other books by Bob Brill;

Tales of My Baseball Youth – A child of the 60's

Al Kabul – Home Grown Terrorist

No Barrier – How the Internet Destroyed the World Economy

Fan Letters to a Stripper – A Patti Waggin Tale (Schiffer Publishing, 2009)

About the author:

Bob Brill is an award winning journalist with over 40 years' experience in radio, media and as a writer. He has written several books including the novel; *"Al Kabul; Home Grown Terrorist,"* and his early memoirs *"Tales of My Baseball Youth; a child of the 60's."* His *"Lancer; Hero of the West"* series of western novels depicts the life and times of a fictional 1880's gun-for-hire who works for the law, not against it. Brill has covered every kind of story from U.S. Presidents to Hollywood entertainment and sports. As a National Correspondent with the UPI Radio Network to local radio stations including the Los Angeles market, he has pretty much done it all. However, as he says there is always another adventure around the corner.

He is also a screenwriter who has completed several feature scripts and TV pilots. He has hopes of seeing his first western film script on the big screen soon. An historian by nature he lives by his own code; "Be a student of history, not a victim of it."

www.ingramcontent.com/pod-product-compliance
Lightning Source LLC
Chambersburg PA
CBHW020636180626
46816CB00003B/989